REGINA RUDD
MERRICK

To Sue —
Enjoy a taste of
Cutlender Co.!
Regina Merrick
Ps 37:4

To my parents, Richard and Wanda Rudd.
You instilled in me a love of home from day one, and were never
afraid to try something just because it was hard.

Welcome to

THE MOSAIC COLLECTION

———————∕∿∕———————

We are sisters, a beautiful mosaic united by the love of God through the blood of Christ.

Each month The Mosaic Collection releases one faith-based novel or anthology exploring our theme, Family by His Design, and sharing stories that feature diverse, God-designed families. All are contemporary stories ranging from mystery and women's fiction to comedic and literary fiction. We hope you'll join our Mosaic family as we explore together what truly defines a family.

If you're like us, loneliness and suffering have touched your life in ways you never imagined; but Dear One, while you may feel alone in your suffering—whatever it is—you are never alone!

Subscribe to *Grace & Glory*, the official newsletter of The Mosaic Collection, to receive monthly encouragement from Mosaic authors, as well as timely updates about events, new releases, and giveaways.

Learn more about The Mosaic Collection at
www.mosaiccollectionbooks.com

Join our Reader Community, too!
www.facebook.com/groups/TheMosaicCollection

Books in

THE MOSAIC COLLECTION

———⁓———

Learn more at www.mosaiccollectionbooks.com/books

There is no fear in love; but perfect love casts out all fear, because fear involves torment. But he who fears has not been made perfect in love. We love Him because He first loved us.

1 John 4:18-19

1

JULY

"Del Reno, I could kill you." Walking up to the front porch of the dilapidated farmhouse, Lisa Reno finally let out the huge sigh that seemed to engulf her.

When her brother broke his leg the week before, she should have canceled all their upcoming Reno Renovations projects.

But no. She had to be the super-sister. After all, she was a designer, wasn't she? She could figure out this contractor stuff. Didn't she help him make all the most important decisions, anyway? In the heat of the moment, she was invincible. In the cold light of day, she knew she was in over her head.

Sure, she had building cred. She had watched more home improvement than most girls her age. A degree in interior design and a DIY résumé that went back to watching Bob Vila from her daddy's lap should be worth something. Shouldn't it?

Yes and no. She closed her eyes and shook her head. The last thing she needed was the local contracting community regarding her as "Daddy's little girl." She was twenty-seven years old and a partner in a design/build firm with her father and brother. And yet, around here she knew everyone thought of her as that redheaded, freckle-faced daughter of Steve Reno, and one of these days everyone would find out she was nothing more than that.

Better go in and see what she'd gotten herself into. She started taking mental notes. Windows to be replaced or restored. Porch floor to be replaced. Pull off the aging vinyl siding and see what was under there. Rip off the dull aluminum trim. That was the worst.

But then she saw the landscaping. Gotta love plastic flowers stuck in the ground. It was springtime year round here, it seemed. She looked again and laughed. Nope. It was Christmas year round. The plastic flowers were faded poinsettias.

Better to laugh than cry, Mama used to say.

If Lisa were on one of those renovation shows she enjoyed, this would be where the door opened and the host would laugh about how nasty it was. Then they would point out this and that feature that could be highlighted. They'd have a computer rendering of their vision for the entire property on hand. In less than an hour, the new homeowners would be amazed as they were led on a tour of a completely renovated house, inside and out.

From experience, she knew that those one-hour renovations took months to complete. And this one? This one looked as if it could take years.

Standing inside the foyer of the 1910 Craftsman farmhouse, she noted mounds of trash—holding who-knew-what kind of vermin nests—sagging stairs, uneven floors, layers of wallpaper, and cracked ceiling plaster.

And the smell. She couldn't quite put her finger on it.

It was so nasty that when she felt a vibration, she almost jumped out of her skin, thinking a critter had made its way into her pocket.

When she saw "BigBroDel" flash on the screen, she shook her head before pushing the button to open the face-to-face call. There was her brother's face, a little worse for wear.

"Del, you scared me to death."

"What did I do?" He seemed as confused by her attitude as she was by the enormity of this project.

"Never mind. Have you actually been in this house?" She continued walking through the lower floor. "There is junk everywhere. It's a trash heap. Look at this stuff." She turned the phone so he could get a good sense of the magnitude of the job.

He laughed. "Ah, sis, it's a jewel in the rough."

"'Rough' being the operative word here."

"Yeah, I was in there with the owner right after he bought it. I planned to get out there yesterday to start clearing out the debris, but you know how that worked out." He shrugged his shoulders and grinned at her.

She took a deep breath. "I know. Sorry. I didn't mean to whine, but you could have warned me about the smell in here."

He winked at her on the screen. "No worries. I'm used to the whining. I didn't notice anything stinky last time I was there, but it's been a while."

"Either it's a recent addition to the ambiance, or you're sniffer needs to be checked." She walked into the kitchen. "The light is magnificent in here." She showed him the full bank of windows facing into the back yard. "Did this used to be a back porch or something?"

"I don't think so. I think they were smart enough, even back then, to know that summer in the South means you need lots and lots of windows to open—especially in the kitchen."

"I can work with this. The rest of it? I don't know." She crept up the stairs and gave him a dirty look. "Squeaky, much?"

"Easy fix."

"Easy for you."

"Hey, you said, and I quote, 'I can handle it. You just get well.'"

She turned the phone toward her face and stuck out her tongue. "I lied. You were pitiful and I felt sorry for you. And besides, since when do you listen to me?"

"Since I didn't have a choice." He grimaced. She could tell he was in pain.

She wrinkled her nose in sympathy. "Have you taken your pain meds?"

"I had some Ibuprofen. I'm saving the hard stuff for bedtime, so I can sleep."

"Good idea. Don't let the pain get too bad before you take something." She worried about him.

He steered clear of painkillers. She and Del had both seen too many of their friends, sidelined by injuries, hooked on medications to get them through the pain. When Del let God get involved in his life, he was all-in, and he wanted to keep it that way.

"I won't. Listen, I didn't just call to get a look at the house. I wanted to let you know I got a licensed contractor to help you out on this. You'll still be in charge, but he knows about annoying things like moving walls, leveling floors, and so on."

She contemplated the space around her and noticed that her shoulders were slumping more the longer she looked at the project before her. "Probably a good idea. Are you sure you don't want to let them find another company to take care of it?"

"I would, but they literally couldn't find anyone else that would tackle it."

"And what makes you think this guy will?" She hoped her glare was translating through the telephone camera.

"He owes me." Her brother grinned. "And he should be arriving any minute now."

Nick Woodward parked at the barn and walked around the property. He told his buddy Del that, under the circumstances, he would be glad to step in and help on this project. It was important to him, too.

Who knew a random 'I owe you' would turn into a monumental project, and this particular monumental project, at that. He walked back around to the front of the house and saw a pickup truck. The magnetic sign on the truck read 'Reno-Vations–Re-Do it Right.'

Typical Del. When they went to college together, they were both English literature and composition majors. So what do two guys with English majors and no teaching credentials do when they get out of college? They become contractors, of course.

Del had the right idea. His sister was a design major, and his dad had been a contractor for years. When Steve Reno decided to semi-retire, he passed the legacy of Reno Construction on to his kids. Del must have added the tag line, homage to his literary studies; alliteration was Del's first love.

A young lady holding her phone in front of her walked out the front door and onto the porch. She looked up from her call when she saw him coming toward her, waving her fingers. Her eyes widened with recognition.

Was that Lisa? He couldn't tell. He hadn't seen her since college. She'd been a couple of years behind them, so while he was living the high life of an upper-classman, she was keeping her nose to the grindstone taking classes and doing whatever it was artsy people did in their spare time. From what he remembered, she had looked fifteen at twenty, was somewhat mousy, and was constantly pushing her glasses up on her nose that was perpetually stuck in a book of some kind.

There was always something about her, though, that drew him. After he got to know her a little better, through Del, flirting with her on the quad at Murray State became a habit, and she usually rolled her eyes and ignored him.

He caught himself raking his hand through his unruly hair. He needed a haircut. Looking down, he noticed the dried concrete on his boots he hadn't noticed before. He could have at least put on his better pair, but it wasn't like he wanted to impress anybody. It was his skills as a contractor they were depending on, not his appearance.

He glanced up and saw her hold up a finger indicating she'd just be a minute. Nodding, he couldn't help but watch as she walked around the corner of the wrap-around porch.

While he waited, he decided to take a closer look at the front porch. Spongy wood in places. Great. That didn't bode well. Chances were they would end up ripping the whole porch off and starting over. More expense. This was why he dealt mainly with new construction.

"Nick?"

It was her. Come on. Could seven years make this much difference? He remembered the auburn hair, but not the brilliant green eyes. "Lisa?"

She looked surprised, and a little flushed as she held out her hand and smiled. "I didn't think you would remember me."

He took her slender hand in his, surprised by the confident grip in such a soft hand. "Sure I remember you. I almost..."

"Didn't recognize me? I know. I get it all the time." She shrugged. "No glasses." She wrinkled her nose and laughed. "I wonder why Del didn't tell me the contractor he'd hired was you."

He lifted an eyebrow and smiled back, wondering the same thing. So Del hadn't told her who the owner was.

"Whatever his reason, it's good to see you."

"And you."

Was that a slight blush on her face, or was it getting hot out here?

Rather than continue standing there awkwardly, both turned to face the house. "Looks like he's tasked us with this gem of a place." He glanced over at her. Her eyes were narrowed, and she had her index finger tapping on her chin as she gazed upon the dilapidated structure.

"He called it a 'jewel in the rough.'" She glanced at him. "You know, the more I look at it, the more I agree with him."

"You're so solemn about it." He hoped his half grin came off the way he intended.

"It's a big job." She stared a few seconds more. "But it'll be worth it. With acreage, people will be jumping to buy this place."

"Maybe. Or maybe it won't be for sale."

She glanced at him in surprise. "Really? I thought this was a flip project?"

"Nope. Renovation and restoration, as much as possible." He put his hands in his pockets and stretched his shoulders as he took a deep breath. He spoke quietly. "This is a special place."

She tilted her head. "Special, how?"

A wave of sadness engulfed him. "It was my grandparents' place. My dad grew up here." Not that he cared. Until Granny died, his father, Dan Woodward, hadn't set foot on the place any more than he had to.

But Nick missed his grandmother. She was gone when he lost Kristy, and he knew she would have known the right things to say. He needed to let go of the past and get on with the job at hand.

"Seriously?" Her mouth dropped open. "Not only did Del not tell me you were the contractor, but he also didn't tell me his 'buddy' was the owner."

"Yeah. I bought it. It went out of the family about ten years ago, when my grandmother passed. The most recent owner lost it to the bank, and I was able to get it back. As for the work, I thought it would be better to hire it out, time-wise, so I asked Del to do it for me."

"Hence, 'I owe you' came back to roost."

"Exactly." He dragged the word out. He considered himself a good contractor, but this was one project he didn't want to mess up. His dad might not agree that it was a good idea to keep the place, but he hadn't asked his opinion.

"Alrighty, then, owner-contractor, that makes you the boss of this job." She saluted him.

He shook his head. "Nope. Your company, your crew. I'll work alongside the lead carpenter and work with you on making decisions. How does that sound?"

"It sounds...complicated."

2

"Penny for your thoughts?"

Crud. She'd forgotten for a moment she wasn't alone. Her college crush was right there, by her side, standing in front of his house. She closed her eyes for a fraction of a second to get her thoughts back in order. He was the same Nick Woodward as the last time she saw him, but a little older, a little sadder. And wearing a wedding ring.

"Exterior. What would you like done here?"

"What would you suggest?"

She twisted her lips to one side. He might not want to hear what she would suggest.

"What's the budget?"

He narrowed his eyes. "How big does it need to be?"'

"Depends. If you want a restoration, it'll be one number, a renovation, another number, and not necessarily more or less."

He stared at the house. She figured he was mentally tallying up the difference in his head.

"Tell you what. Before I give you a number, let's go through the house and write down all that needs to be done, and then add it up. We can figure the budget and prioritize from there. How does that sound?"

Smart, that's how it sounds.

She nodded. "Let's start with the exterior."

"All right." He regarded her closely. "Vinyl still looks pretty good."

She closed her eyes. Ugh. No. Not the vinyl. Surely not...Save the argument for the plaster versus drywall scene. She opened her eyes when he started chuckling.

"What's so funny?"

"Your face. It thought you were going to pass out when I said the vinyl looked good." He recovered. "Sorry. I know the vinyl needs to go. No amount of chemicals would whiten the stuff. I want to see what's under there. If it's rotten, we'll put in Hardie siding."

"Bless you, Nick." She could feel her heart start beating again. "I thought I was going to have to fire you from your own house."

"Now that would be awkward, wouldn't it?"

Not as awkward as working side-by-side with my long-lost-totally-unaware-love.

"It would. I'd say the crew could start ripping it off pretty soon. And the porch, too. I hope some of the joists are worth salvaging." She bounced a little on the spongy part of the porch.

When the floorboard broke under her minuscule weight, she went straight down. She stood on the dirt below, waist-deep in porch.

"Darn it! Why do I always find the rotted floorboards?" Muttering under her breath, she gritted her teeth and felt the heat creep up her face. Of all times to have this happen.

Nick sprang into action. "Are you okay?" He reached down to help her climb out without disturbing the boards that were still viable.

"Thanks." She brushed off the debris and stepped away from the new hole in the porch, trying her best to tamp down her temper.

He arched one eyebrow. "Does this happen often?"

"More often than I would prefer. I'm glad I had jeans on this time, instead of shorts. Ouch." She lifted her bootcut pants leg to reveal a nasty bruise and scrape. "Oh well, another one to add to the list."

"Are you sure you're okay?"

She waved a hand in dismissal. "I'm fine. All in a day's work for a klutz." She walked ahead of him into the house, face burning, rubbing her leg as she went.

Great. Score one for the clumsy kid dressing up as a contractor. "Hopefully the smell will go away when we get the trash out of here."

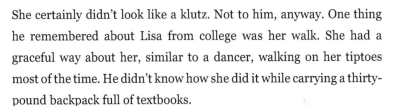

She certainly didn't look like a klutz. Not to him, anyway. One thing he remembered about Lisa from college was her walk. She had a graceful way about her, similar to a dancer, walking on her tiptoes most of the time. He didn't know how she did it while carrying a thirty-pound backpack full of textbooks.

But she had changed. Her tentative step had been replaced with confidence, for the most part. She seemed skittish but handled herself well. She was a professional now, not a self-conscious college student.

"You weren't kidding about the smell." He noticed the piles of garbage in the front room. "Wow." It wasn't eye-watering, but he didn't want to wait too long to get to the bottom of it. Maybe a dead raccoon or rat somewhere in the debris?

"When did you decide to go into business with Del?" According to her brother, they had made a decent go of working together.

"I started working for Dad after my internship."

He appraised the young woman in front of him. "Yeah, Del said something about you being on a TV show."

She chuckled. "I wasn't exactly on it, but it gave me a better idea of what this business looks like when it's not your family." She sighed. "And how to be camera-ready in case you get caught in the background."

"Got caught unprepared?"

"Once. After seeing myself on television, I made friends with the hair and makeup folks and learned a few tips—and got contacts." She shook her head. "I'll put it this way. This wasn't my first trip through a floor."

He threw back his head and laughed. It felt good. Not many reasons to laugh lately. He sensed a little tension but felt relaxed at the same time. "We'll make sure it doesn't happen again. So you came back home after that?"

She paused. "Yeah. Mom was sick. They offered me a job to stay, but I wanted to get home. Then when she died, I decided to stick around to help out, and here I am." She grinned. "I guess for an introvert, it wasn't a bad way to get started in the business. I didn't even have to put together a résumé." She shrugged and smiled. "After a while, Dad made me talk to the contractors working under him when I wanted something done, and I discovered that when I was calling the shots, I wasn't as painfully shy as I thought."

"I get it. I started out with a local contractor, building new homes. I discovered I was pretty good at it, and finally branched out on my own."

They continued walking through the house, taking notes as they went.

She glanced over at him, cheeks pinker than before. "I've heard good things about your company."

Nick raised his eyebrows and smiled as they walked through the kitchen door. "Thanks. I hear you guys are good, too."

She smiled back. "Thanks. Del does a good job. We love the old stuff." She turned toward the kitchen. "And this is definitely old stuff. Especially the odor. Sometimes old houses come with surprises." She waved her hand in front of her nose and then stopped to spread her arms, taking in the bank of windows. "I have a couple of ideas for the kitchen."

"Buy stock in air freshener? Move it to a different location? Add on?"

"Maybe yes on the air freshener, but moving it? Good grief no. I love it where it is. It catches the sun on two sides. And if we take out this wall and put in an island it will get sun from three sides, the dining room will get sun from the kitchen, and you'll have more of an open concept." She grinned. "It would be a win-win. But you're the boss."

He pondered the wall situation for a minute. "That could work. It would cost more—I'll have to see if we'd need a structural beam there, and then whether it came down or was up in the ceiling would make a difference, but it's a definite possibility."

She nodded. "Otherwise, you're stuck with a tiny kitchen. Nobody wants that, these days."

"Tell me about it. Kitchens and bathrooms. It's what the people want." He arched an eyebrow. "Speaking of which, what are the bathrooms like? I have a vague recollection of a tiny one on the first floor and a bigger one on the second."

Lisa grimaced. "You recollect correctly." She led him down a small hallway at the back of the house. "This is the downstairs bath." She pointed to the tiny room next to it. "The bathroom and this little room were once a porch. By the style of the sink and tub, I'd say they converted it into a bathroom in the '40s or '50s, and I doubt that it was constructed to have a shower."

"I remember the plastic tile." He chuckled when one popped off and fell into the tub. "There used to be a tube of marine epoxy in the medicine cabinet to keep them glued on." He opened the mirrored unit above the sink. "Two bandages and an empty aspirin bottle."

"I guess the people who owned it last decided not to bother." She pointed to the scattering of the gray plastic squares in the tub and in various places on the floor. "I suggest a gut job, maybe a walk-in shower instead of a tub-shower unit."

"My thoughts exactly." He followed her through the house and up the stairs.

His mind raced back in time to himself as a little boy running up and down the stairs. He had good times here. It had upset him when they sold it, but at the time, he was in college and in no position to hang on to it. Dad seemed all too eager to unload the place.

They checked the bedrooms and closets. Cosmetic work, mostly: refinish floors, paint, repair plaster. There were lots of windows to replace, but the amount of natural light made it worthwhile.

"Here's the second bathroom. Nice and big, but no counter space." She looked up at him.

"One sink in here is not acceptable. We'll gut this one, too. How much do you think?" He trusted her judgment even more than he thought he would. He still couldn't get over little Lisa Reno being this confident, well-spoken designer. There was the porch incident, but everyone has a little klutz in them.

"Depends on how deep a gut. Del says there's a chimney going through the house from the basement up. If we take it out, we could expand this room, or even get a second bath up here if we stole square footage from the hall closet." Her eyes were shining at the thought.

"I'll keep it in mind. Sounds a little scary." It sounded more than a little scary. It sounded like an impossible task, and expensive, but she seemed to think it would be doable. He'd talk to Del about it. They took a turn through the upstairs bedrooms and closets, and then began the descent down the squeaking staircase.

"Speaking of scary…"

He turned a quizzical face toward her. "Scary?"

"Yes, scary. We haven't seen the basement yet."

"Oh, I've seen it, but it's been years. I seem to recall it being the kind of basement that shows up in a horror movie."

She twisted her lips nervously. "Let's get it over with. You know, in a movie, when the main character is creeping down the squeaky steps, I'm the one yelling at them not to go into the basement." She paused in thought. "Or the attic. I've had nightmares about attics."

He laughed as she shivered at the basement doorway. "I'll protect you. Ready?"

She sighed. "Ready as I'll ever be. I haven't been down here. Del came and checked it out."

Nick opened the door and the smell made him pause, almost knocking him to his knees. "Whatever it is, it's down there."

"Great." She scrunched her nose. "I wish I had a particulate mask with me."

He pulled a bandana out of his pocket. "This is clean. You want it?"

"Thanks. I don't know if it will help, but we need to get whatever is stinking OUT of there before we can work on the house."

"Watch the first step." He spoke as she went down further on the top step than she anticipated.

She frowned up at him. "Thanks for the warning."

"Sorry. It's actually worse than when I was here last."

"Oh my goodness." This was ridiculously funky. And not in a decorative way.

"Yeah." He held his nose and reviewed the underground room.

It wasn't that there was so much stuff in the basement, but the type of stuff. "Is it just me, or are there are a lot of old appliances down here?" Lisa scanned the area in confusion.

"Three washers, two dryers, and an electric range." Nick put his hand on the brick chimney in the middle of the basement, looking at it and shaking his head. "That's gonna be a bear to take down."

"Yeah. It goes through the kitchen, too, but it would be part of opening it up to get the open-concept floor plan." She grinned. She so wanted to get her way on this one.

"I don't know." Nick walked around the basement, studying the brick foundation covered in concrete. "I'll bet it leaks like a sieve."

"Probably. All this is really good for is storage, but it's good space."

"Do you see anything to account for the smell down here?" He was checking all the nooks and crannies, as was she. Nothing.

She followed him to the back corner, where he had stopped on his inspection. "What have you found?"

He pointed at a section of the wall with new concrete. "This is odd. When I was a kid, there was always a big cabinet here. I figured it was built in."

"Maybe the foundation wall failed?" She pondered as he felt along the edges of the gray concrete. It was a stark contrast to the white paint on the rest of the basement walls.

"I don't think so. The cabinet was still here when Del and I came down here a few months ago, when I first bought the place." He shook his head and glanced at her with a frown. "And it didn't smell like this then, either. There has to be something..." He glanced around and picked up an old screwdriver lying on the floor with some other discarded tools. He started scraping in one spot at the edge, finally revealing wood, not brick.

"What is it?" Her eyes widened as she stared at him.

He glanced at her and continued scraping. "Get another tool and start on the other side. I have an idea."

All she saw was a hammer. "Wait a minute. I have a five-in-one tool in the truck. Be right back."

"You just want to get outside where you can breathe."

"You're not wrong." She ran up the stairs to the rear door and returned with her toolbox in record time.

"I admire a girl who's prepared."

"Always. Girl Scout motto." She handed him a mask she retrieved from the truck. It didn't help much, but it was better than nothing, and it left their hands free.

"I thought that was Boy Scouts?"

She bit her bottom lip and started digging into the concrete on the other side. It came off easier when she found the spot right where the old concrete and bricks met the new. She laughed, concentrating on her task. "Both."

"Ah. I'll have to watch my step around you."

"Why's that?"

He chuckled. "I think you're smarter than I am."

She glanced over at him, feeling the heat rise to her face as she saw his eyes crinkle, his grin hidden by the mask. "I think you'll be okay."

"Look at this." He brushed off the extra debris and stood back.

Her eyes widened once more, and the hair rose on the nape of her neck as she stared into his deep brown eyes. "Is that a door?"

3

Nick almost smiled when he saw the gooseflesh on Lisa's arms. There were many things he didn't expect to happen today. A mystery door in the basement was only one of them. Seeing a decidedly grown-up Lisa Reno was another.

"I would say it's definitely a door." He searched around to see if any tools were lying about. His toolbox was in the truck and, until now, he hadn't noticed the case she brought down with her earlier. As if reading his mind, she handed him a prybar. "Thanks."

"I didn't want to go back out to the truck." She shrugged and stood next to him as he tried to pry the door loose.

"Looks like it hasn't been sealed up too long." He tapped at the concrete with the tool in his hand. "It was too easy to remove. A good cement job wouldn't have crumbled like this."

"If you're trying to get hired, you've got the job." Lisa laughed at his serious expression.

He glanced up at her from his position bent over to loosen the bottom of the door, arching an eyebrow. "Concrete porosity is important, but I'm glad they didn't do a good job on this one." He did one final yank, and the door budged, sending a spray of dust and debris over them as it opened. They stood, side-by-side, peering into the darkness, reeling from the wave of odors. It almost made him rethink their exploration.

"What is it?" Her watering eyes were wide with wonder. "A secret room? Maybe a tunnel?"

Nick pushed away the cobwebs in the doorway. "There's a breeze coming from inside."

She handed him her flashlight and put both hands over her face. "Unfortunately, the breeze isn't helping. Are you sure you want to go in there? I'm not sure how much more I can take."

"I'll go alone if you want me to."

She attempted to take a deep breath but stopped and shook her head instead. "I'll go." He could imagine the war inside her head–to face whatever was in there or get out of here as quickly as possible. "You first."

"And I was always taught, 'ladies first.'"

Lisa shook her head furiously. "I'll forego the niceties this time if you don't mind."

He took the flashlight and turned it on. "Right. Are you Nancy Drew, or am I one of the Hardy Boys?" He shined the light into the blackness, checking the ceiling, floor, and walls. Nothing but a single light bulb hanging from the ceiling, and it looked ancient.

Lisa pulled the chain attached to the light but got no response. "The flashlight will have to do. Wait a minute." She stopped to dig into her pocket, then pulled out her keys, complete with a key-chain flashlight. "I have this little one, too. And you're showing your age. Maybe Bones and Booth?"

He was enjoying this, and it was unexpected. He hadn't felt this comfortable with a woman since...well, in a long time. "Considering the odors in this house, that might be more realistic. Plus, I knew you wanted to be the smart one."

"Can't deny what's true." She was systematically scanning her surroundings.

She knelt down. "Look at this."

Kneeling next to her, he flooded the item with the larger flashlight. "Whatever it is, it's old." He picked up the piece of rusted metal and put it in his pocket. "I'll check it later, aboveground."

They continued to follow the light and the smell coming from somewhere down the dark path.

"Are you still back there?"

"You couldn't get rid of me that easily." She was going to stick as close to him as possible. It wasn't exactly that she was scared, more that she wasn't fond of tight spaces in the dark. *Especially* in the dark. There was something ominous about creeping along with the smell of death all around them.

Nick continued on, his flashlight shining on the floor, the walls, and the ceiling, to make sure they didn't run into anything.

Or anyone.

When he stopped abruptly, Lisa plowed right into his solid back.

"Sorry. Tree root." He shone the light around a slightly larger area. "Lisa, look over there."

His flashlight jiggled in the direction he wanted her to look. "Is that..."

She jumped and screamed when she felt something cross her foot. Her voice shook. "I don't know what is over there, but I'm pretty sure I just felt a rat walk over my foot."

She stood there, her eyes closed in near panic. When Nick tightened his hand on her arm, she felt him shaking. Were they in danger?

"Lisa. Open your eyes."

She did and peeked down at the furry creature next to her foot. Then another, and another. She looked up at Nick to see him laughing. "I think you're safe."

There were five kittens, two calicoes, one gray-striped, one black, and one marmalade, all being herded to safety by their mother, a gray tabby cat.

"Oh my goodness. How did they get in here?" She held her hand out to the mother cat, but there was no way the cat was going to trust a human who almost stepped on her children. What was she thinking? "They're so sweet."

"I guess they got in from the other end. It's for sure they didn't come in from the basement as we did." He walked ahead and started toward his original focus, leaving her to admire the kittens. "I'm afraid we may have a bit of a problem.

"What kind of problem?"

He focused his flashlight on a mound of material in the corner, and they both walked toward it.

Her hands flew to her face, glad of the mask she wore. A scream lodged in her throat as the realization took hold that the object in the corner had the distinct shape of something she'd never encountered in any old house she'd ever inspected.

A body.

4

There was now no question as to the source of the smell permeating the house, and very possibly their pores, but at this point the smell was the least of Nick's concern. Was this really a body? His brain was having a hard time wrapping itself around the concept. He didn't want it to be, but as he drew closer he could see the top of a man's head. And then there was the putrid smell of decay. There was no getting around that.

"Nick..." She grabbed his arm, clutching him like a lifeline, but he was still so stunned he almost didn't feel it. Almost.

"Stay here, Lisa." He walked toward the mound of cloth that he now knew was a corpse. But how long had it been there? It was covered with an old rug, perhaps pulled from the previous section of the basement, under the house. He turned toward her. "I guess I have to look, don't I?"

"Well, I'm not." Her voice shook, bringing a slight grin to his shocked face.

"Here goes nothin'." He focused his light at the top of the corpse's head and walked slowly toward it. The closer he got the more blood he could see. There was a pool of dried blood beneath the man's head.

"What do you see?"

"Blood. Lots of it."

"Do you think...?"

"I think his head was smashed in."

He heard her back away.

"It's not fresh. We need to call the sheriff." He pointed the flashlight beam around the room they had found. "I don't think he tripped and fell over a cat."

"Are you sure? I mean, maybe it was an accident?"

"Then who covered it up with a rug?"

She was silent.

He turned the light upward so they could see one another. "We need to get out of here."

She looked down at her phone. "I've got the sheriff's number, but there's no signal down here."

He nodded. "Let's get above ground."

"You won't get any argument from me."

She followed behind him with precision, but they left faster than they had entered. "This might change a few things in the renovation."

"You think?"

Her sarcasm was welcome. Anything to get rid of the image of a decaying corpse and a pool of blood in his basement.

They made their way back through the recently-unearthed door and to welcome light, sucking in as much oxygen as they could. He looked back at her. "Are you okay?"

"I will be. Not every day a house inspection turns into a murder mystery."

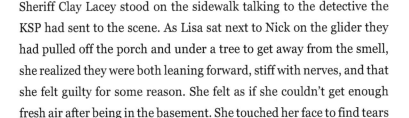

Sheriff Clay Lacey stood on the sidewalk talking to the detective the KSP had sent to the scene. As Lisa sat next to Nick on the glider they had pulled off the porch and under a tree to get away from the smell, she realized they were both leaning forward, stiff with nerves, and that she felt guilty for some reason. She felt as if she couldn't get enough fresh air after being in the basement. She touched her face to find tears there. Were they from the eye-watering stench or from the overwhelming desire to run as far and as fast from here as her feet could take her?

She noted the sickened expression on Nick's face that she was sure mirrored her own.

"Are you okay?" He seemed to focus on her fully, for the first time since they emerged from the house.

"In shock, I think." She shivered in the July heat. "What happened down there?"

He gazed out over the field across the road and shook his head. "I have no idea. Is it crazy to feel guilty because a corpse was found inside my house?"

She nodded. "I was thinking the same thing. Conditioned response from watching too many cop shows?"

"Probably." He gave her a half grin, noting that Clay had bid the detective adieu and was pulling an ancient rocker over to them. "But how long was he down there?"

"We won't know for sure until the coroner gets back to us." Clay sat, then checked beneath him at a loud creaking sound.

Lisa held her breath a moment as he made sure it would stand his six foot six, two hundred fifty-pound weight.

"Are you okay, Lisa?" Clay's piercing blue eyes held hers for a moment.

She smiled at her former classmate. "I'm fine. Just a little rattled." She was too hard on him. The last date they had wasn't so bad. Well, until it was. She focused when Nick began to talk.

"They had to have come in from the tunnel or the basement, then probably went back and sealed off the entrance from the basement." Nick leaned forward, hands clasped between his knees.

Clay looked at his notes, then up at Nick. He looked angry. "That's what I figure. I'd say he's been there for a while. We'd know more if you hadn't disturbed the crime scene. How close did you get to the body?"

Nick shook his head. "Close enough to see that the blood on the floor was dried. After that, we got out of there."

"And then we called you." Lisa folded her arms across her chest, trying to keep her shaking to a minimum.

"The house is off-limits until forensics finishes dusting for prints and checking for the other end of the tunnel."

Lisa shivered. The regional medical examiner's office staff came out the front door with the corpse encased in a black body bag. After the initial response, the first thing she thought of was opening every window in the house to get the smell out. There was part of her that was glad she wouldn't have to enter the house for a while.

Clay was still talking, and she was missing it. "Any ideas, Mr. Woodward?"

"I never even knew there was a tunnel. Neither my grandmother nor my dad ever mentioned it. As I told Lisa, there was always a big piece of furniture in front of where the door was. When I saw it was gone, at first I figured the last owners decided to get rid of the stuff that was there before they came, along with their own stuff."

"Did you know the former owners?" Clay didn't look up while he wrote on his notepad.

"No, I bought it from the bank."

Clay nodded and continued looking down at his notes. "I can check into that."

"I don't want to be insensitive, but since the body is gone, can someone go down and rescue the cat and kittens?" Lisa took a deep cleansing breath. Maybe if she drew in enough oxygen now, she wouldn't have to breathe while she went in there. Tiny furry creatures would be the only thing that could entice her to go back down there.

Clay shook his head and grinned. "Should have known you'd be more worried about a stray and a bunch of kittens than preserving a crime scene."

Lisa sighed. Clay knew her too well, and for way too long. "I'm pretty sure you can't pin the murder on a tabby and five kittens."

"You never know. The officers may be questioning them now." Clay winked at her, causing her to feel heat rush up her neck. Bad timing. A few dates with him and he thought he could tease her the way he did when they were kids riding the school bus together.

"Very funny. Maybe somebody can take a picture of you rescuing the kittens and put it on your re-election Facebook page."

A thoughtful expression crossed his face, then he seemed to dismiss it. "No, but when we get more facts, a mysterious corpse in a hidden tunnel wouldn't be a bad plug."

"How long do you think the crime scene will be active? We were in the process of inspecting the house when the mystery found us." Nick seemed a little impatient, which was understandable, but a little cold-hearted at the same time. Had he forgotten a man had died down there? But, it was his house, after all.

Clay stood and looked at both of them. "Nick, I'll call you as soon as I know. The KSP is taking the lead on this, and I'll be lucky if I get any part of it."

"Noted."

Lisa stopped him before he got away. "Did I hear you say the crime scene unit from KSP would be here in the morning?"

He halfway pivoted toward her. "Yeah. The body's going to the forensic lab in Madisonville, and some of the evidence will go to the central lab in Lexington. Forensics from Madisonville should be here first thing in the morning, so stay out of there until they're done. I'll be here, so I'll let you know." He walked down to the sidewalk and stopped to point his finger at her. "Kittens or no kittens, keep away from the crime scene, you hear?"

"I hear." Lisa twisted her lips in a disgusted frown. Her mind switched to the practical. How could they get the smell out? She had a feeling it was more than a simple Google search could handle. Not that she really wanted to go into the house for a while. Tomorrow, maybe. Hopefully not by herself, and if she could help it, she might never go in the basement again.

"That escalated quickly." Nick elicited a soft sigh from the redhead sitting next to him.

The sheriff and deputies drove off, leaving them alone.

"Not your typical, run-of-the-mill property inspection, for sure." Lisa twisted her lips and shook her head. "Del will be sorry he missed all the excitement."

"When I told him I owed him, I had no idea." He leaned forward, his elbows on his knees as he considered his property from under the tree in the front yard. "It's peaceful again."

Lisa chuckled. "Finally." She looked around, too. "It's nice to smell the fresh air and hear the birds and frogs."

He turned and grinned at her. "Don't forget the crickets."

"Ah yes, the inimitable cricket. It's my favorite sound on my white noise app." As soon as she said it, she wondered why she would admit to something so lame. Nerves. Anything rather than talk about the elephant in the room—or the body in the basement.

"You have a white noise app?"

Shrugging, she pulled out her phone and demonstrated it. "Hey, it was free, and if I'm not at home, I can't sleep. Sometimes I turn it on just because I like it."

"Cool. I'll have to try it. Although I've never been accused of being a light sleeper. At least I used to be able to sleep. Not so much now."

She had heard. Del was better at keeping up with his friends than she was, although Nick had always fallen under the category of "Del's friend" rather than hers. It wasn't right for someone to go through so much pain. Not like that, anyway.

"I'm sorry about your wife, Nick." She glanced over at him, meeting his eyes briefly. She saw a wince of pain before he cleared his expression. The mask came back down.

"Thanks. It was tough, but life goes on. I hated to hear about your mom. I was out of pocket when she died, or I would have been there."

She nodded. Del had told her that Nick's wife was killed two days before their mom died. She had lost her mother, but it wasn't the same. This brush with death brought it all back but in a horrifying way. The glimpse she'd gotten of the corpse was more than she wanted to remember. Nick had experienced it full-on.

Nick cleared his throat and straightened. "Anyway, enough of that. Let's talk house and when we can get started."

Lisa swallowed the lump in her throat. *Focus.* She stood and walked toward the house, then stopped front and center to review the exterior again. "While we've got good weather, I'd suggest we tackle the siding and roof first. Get it weather-tight before the fall rain starts in. What do you think?" Her voice sounded shaky, even to her.

Nodding thoughtfully, he walked down and stood beside her on the sidewalk. "I agree." He stuffed his hands in his pockets and glanced at her before putting his attention back on the elevation of the house. "You'll have to bear with me. I'm used to being the boss."

"And you'll have to bear with me. I'm used to bossing the boss. In my case, it's usually my brother."

5

After going home and showering to within an inch of her life, Lisa drove to her brother's house. She knew it was an ordeal for him to come to the door, so when she unlocked it to smell wonderful aromas coming from the region of his kitchen, she paused. Someone was cooking.

"Hello?"

"We're back here, sis."

She made her way through the mid-century modern semi-open-concept living and dining room. Her brother sat at the kitchen table, orthopedic-boot-clad foot resting on another chair, grinning like the cat that swallowed the canary.

Lisa stood there, hands on her hips. "I had a feeling."

"About what?"

Roxy Emerson, the owner of the local diner and their soon-to-be stepmother, was at the stove, stirring a large pot of jambalaya. While stirring, she opened the oven to check on her baking.

Lisa went over to kiss her on the cheek after whacking Del on the back of the head. "I had a feeling all Del had to do was suggest he was the least bit hungry or lonely, and you'd be here. Where's your car?"

"Injured party, here. You might hold off on the whacking and criticizing." Del rubbed the back of his head. "You never did know your own strength."

"Poor baby." She stuck out her tongue at the patient.

"Your dad dropped me off and went to the pharmacy to fill Del's prescription and pick up ice cream to go with the cobbler." Roxy pushed her brunette hair behind her ear and focused on her fully, concern in her glance. "Are you all right?"

"I'm fine. It's been a rough day." She tried to summon a smile but felt her lips quiver. What she wouldn't give for a hug from Mom right now.

"You're pale." Roxy put down her spoon and laid a hand to Lisa's cheeks and forehead. "You don't feel feverish."

She grinned and felt her eyes water slightly. "We ran into a little bit of trouble at the house. I'll tell you all about it later when Dad gets here."

"Are you sure?" Roxy appeared unconvinced.

Lisa nodded and scrutinized her brother in concern. "Are you taking your meds?"

"No, I asked the doc to give me something less narcotic." He handed her the bottle of pills that would be worth a lot of money on a street corner. "Could you drop it by the sheriff's office? I don't even want it in the house."

"Sure. Bad trip, huh?" She grinned, and then sobered when she saw the name of the drug on the label.

"Yeah. It's hard enough to get up when I have to, but when I constantly feel like I need to kill spiders on the wall that aren't there, it's just plain annoying."

"I can only imagine."

"Yeah, the imagining part was the trouble." His eyes looked tired. She could see he hadn't slept well. "I didn't even mention the snakes."

"Ouch. That would be where I got off." She shook the almost-full bottle. "I'm sure I'll be seeing Clay Lacey pretty soon anyway."

"Do you have another date with him?" Roxy pulled the peach cobbler out of the oven, sending the amazing aroma and mouthwatering sweetness into the room. "I thought it didn't go so well last time."

Del was shaking with laughter. "If she goes out with Clay again, I'll eat my hat."

"Don't worry. You can stick to Roxy's cooking. Dating Clay was the low point of my adulthood."

"Now Lisa, you shouldn't say that. He's a nice young man."

"I may have overstated it a bit. In high school he was awkward, and I felt a little sorry for him. When he finished growing and got somewhat good-looking, he became arrogant—but still awkward. I'm surprised he can fit his head into his sheriff's hat." She sighed. "Winning the sheriff's election at such a young age was not good for him."

Del nodded. "He seems to be competent, though."

"And that's all well and good, but I don't want to be involved. Anyway, I met Nick to go through the house today." She paused to glare at her brother. "Why didn't you tell me the 'buddy' you hired was Nick?"

"I figured you'd forgotten all about him." Del quirked an eyebrow at her. "Is there something you'd like to share? You mentioned some trouble."

Flustered, Lisa shook her head. "No, but we did find a little something in the basement we weren't prepared for."

"What? I went through it when he bought it and we didn't find anything."

"Yeah, well, you didn't dig deep enough." She paused for effect. "We found a tunnel."

"Seriously? A tunnel?" Del sat up straight and put all his attention on Lisa. "Where?"

"In the basement. But that wasn't all. Not by a long shot."

"What else did you find?"

Lisa raised her eyebrow and leveled a stare at her brother. "A body."

Del sat up straighter. "A body? As in, a person?"

"Lisa!" Roxy put her hand to her heart and went straight to her and gave her a hug. "Are you sure you're all right?"

"I'll be fine. It was quite a shock." She let her lip tremble for a second, then bit it. "It was awful." Lisa tilted her head. It was nice to have one up on her big brother, but she'd trade it all for not having seen it. "It's an interesting story."

"Sounds like it." Del expelled the deep breath he had taken. "Goes to show you never know what you'll find in an old house."

Roxy put the lid on the pot of soup and poured herself a cup of coffee. "Can I get you two any coffee?"

"Good grief no, it's sweltering outside." Lisa waved her off.

"It's not in here, and besides, my mother always claimed coffee cooled her down." She took a sip and sighed. "Never figured that out, myself, but I adore it anyway." She came over to the table and sat between the siblings. "Don't tell the story until your dad gets here, or you'll have to start over."

"Don't worry. I wasn't going to."

Del grinned. "He might want to get back in the saddle for this one."

"No way, José. We're leaving on our Alaska cruise in two weeks, and he's all mine, you hear?" When Dad began seeing Roxy last Christmas, the last thing Lisa expected was a marriage proposal by Easter, but she felt like she'd been given the gift of another mom in Roxy.

"Yes, ma'am. I'll try to make it sound less interesting." Lisa winked, and then considered her brother. "So, when were you going to tell me it was Nick who not only is your replacement contractor, but also the owner of the house?"

He shifted his jaw mischievously. "I knew you'd figure it out.

Seems to me like someone—not naming names, of course—had a crush on one Nick Woodward about, oh, seven or eight years ago?"

"Really?" Roxy perked up, coffee notwithstanding. "Why have I not heard about this?"

"Because it was a schoolgirl crush and I'm completely over it. Besides, he's been married and widowed since then. I don't imagine he's been thinking about 'little ole' me.'" She tried to stay busy tracing the wood grain pattern on the kitchen table, wishing she had something more specific to do. "I mean, I haven't seen him since college. Which is strange, come to think of it? It's not like he lives so far away. Did he ever come home with you?"

"No, he never did and he wasn't in school here. I knew him through basketball and FFA. His grandparents lived here, but he was only here in the summertime and holidays. We reconnected in college."

Lisa shrugged. "That explains it. Where was his wife from?"

"Eddyville. They met when she came to Murray for grad school."

"So sad for him to be a widower at such a young age." Roxy cradled her coffee cup and shook her head.

"What happened? I couldn't exactly ask him between dodging cobwebs and talking to the state police."

Del frowned. "She died in a car accident."

"Wow. There's no way to prepare for that." She felt sorrow for a woman she never met, who had married the man of *her* dreams as much as he had been the man of her own.

"As sad as losing his wife was, she was pregnant with their first child."

Tears pricked at Lisa's eyes. Most women these days hesitated to admit it, but the idea of bearing children was something they held close for "someday," at least. "I had no idea."

Del curved his lips downward. "He doesn't say much about it."

It could explain the wall he seemed to put up. "He's a guy, after all." Lisa gave her brother a sad grin. "I told him I'd probably treat him the same as I do you, but maybe I can back off a little."

Del shook his head. "If you do, he'll think you feel sorry for him."

"Well, I do." She gaped at her brother in surprise.

"I know, but guys don't like to see people walking around on eggshells."

She looked at Roxy, who simply shrugged and set down her coffee mug. "Don't look at me. I'll never understand men, and I married one and plan to marry another."

The sun was dipping by the time Nick drove off his grandparents' property. Correction. His property. He was now a property owner in the county his dad's family had settled in the mid-1800s. It wasn't the original Woodward homestead, but it was close.

Crittenden County was small, and it had two things to claim: historical and defunct fluorspar mines, and an enormous deer population.

He remembered his grandmother complaining every summer about their inability to keep deer from raiding their garden. She said she didn't work hard putting it out and keeping the weeds at bay only to feed the deer.

He smiled, thinking about it. He remembered getting up with her early on a summer morning, hoeing the rows of corn, beans, peas, and tomatoes. Helping her put poles in the rows of green beans so they could vine up to the sun. Adding manure for fertilizer after it had set out in a pile for a while and "mellowed," for lack of a better term. It still stunk, but the bounty she kept from the deer was worth it.

The only day of the year Dad would go with them to the farm was Christmas. Christmas dinner at her house was amazing with corn straight from her freezer, canned green beans, and so many other things grown on the farm. His mom and dad had never planted a garden, and lived in a subdivision in Elizabethtown. Dad always said he'd had enough farming in his first eighteen years to last a lifetime, but he always seemed interested to hear his son talk about what he did when he spent weeks at a time on the farm.

Maybe it was in his blood, and he'd never explored it.

Did he want to live in the old house? He certainly didn't want to sell it. Most of his construction work was around the lakes area of Kentucky and Barkley Lakes, which were both less than an hour from the farm.

If Kristy were here, what would she want to do? Would the idea of a corpse found on the property put her off completely?

It was a moot point. When they married, their five-year plan included having a baby and building their own house. A new house, lakefront, with all the bells and whistles. Kristy hadn't grown up on a farm but claimed country-girl status because her family lived next door to a cattle farm. He smiled. She was so much more citified than she thought she was, but then so was he. Just because he'd gotten his hands dirty a few times didn't mean he was a country boy even if he was in the Future Farmers of America.

He drove into the garage of his Kuttawa, KY lake house only to hear barking coming from inside. As soon as he opened the door to the laundry room, he was greeted by the collie-mix that was Minerva. Minnie for short. Kristy had named her Minerva, and it never really stuck.

"Hey, girl, what's going on? Ready to go outside?"

He grabbed a few tennis balls and opened the door to the back yard. He was one of the lucky ones. While he didn't have a lakefront house, he did have a lake view, and he was able to fence in his back yard to keep Minnie in check. He also had great property values and none of the headaches of living directly on the lake.

He threw the first tennis ball, but Minnie was too busy sniffing his clothes to pay attention to playtime. He desperately needed a hot shower. As hot as possible. He didn't want to get used to the smell that seemed to be dissipating but probably wasn't except in his own mind. When the phone in his pocket vibrated, he checked the caller ID. Mom. Sighing, he pushed the button to talk.

"Hey, Mom."

"Hey yourself. How was your day?" She always seemed to think he needed someone to ask him, since he was alone, so she did it every day. Every. Day. He couldn't figure out just how to tell them about what they'd found.

"It was good." He found a seat on the patio where he sat and watched as Minnie barked at some baby birds trying to learn how to fly. "I went to check out the old house today."

"How was it? Last time I was there it needed work." He could hear clanks and clinks as she cooked supper. "Of course that's been a while ago."

"It does, but it's a solid house. I'm glad I was able to get my hands on it."

"How many acres are still with the house?"

"About forty."

"That's a lot to take care of. You're not planning to move out there, are you?"

He paused. If he was lonely here, in a lake community, how lonely would he be on a farm ten miles from town? The little community there on the river couldn't really be called a town. More of a wide spot in the road.

"I'm not sure. Still mulling it over."

"It's pretty out there."

"Yeah, it is. I met with Del's sister today. She works with him as a designer."

"Really?" Her voice perked. "Seems as if I remember meeting her when you and Del graduated. Quiet girl, but wonderful red hair."

He grinned. His mother wanted him to find someone so badly. Maybe so she would be off the hook? No. She was just a mom. She wanted her solo chick to be happy. "She's not so quiet anymore. I was surprised."

"Were you, now?" He could hear the wheels turning in her head.

"Don't get any ideas."

"What ideas? Can't a mother want her only son to be in a relationship with a wonderful girl?" She paused. "And if she's Del's sister, how bad could she be?"

"Noted. She's a nice girl, but we're working together, so don't get any ideas in your head. Besides, she may be dating someone."

"Oh. Well, I'll lay off, but don't miss any opportunities."

"Yes, ma'am." He shook his head. "By the way, we did have a little excitement when we went through the house. Is Dad there? I need to ask him about something in the house."

"He is. Hang on a minute." He heard her calling to his dad. "Dan, could you come in here? Nick wants to ask you something about the old house." She fiddled with the buttons on the phone. "Are you still there? I'm trying to find the speaker button."

"I'm still here." He shook his head and whispered "Good girl" to Minnie when she brought him the first tennis ball.

"Here we are. Nick?" Dan Woodward had a booming voice. He almost didn't need the speaker to be heard.

"Hey, Dad. I went through the old house today with Del's sister. She's his designer."

"Pretty rough? I don't know how the last owners left it, but it needed work when Mother passed and we sold it."

"Not too bad, but I'll make some pretty big changes to the floor plan."

"You're not planning to live there."

Nick could hear the objection in his voice and felt his hackles rise.

Not a question. A statement. Dad had left home at eighteen and didn't go back until Granddad died, except for a few hours on Christmas day. "I told Mom I was still thinking about it. We'll see what happens." He paused. "We did run into a few unexpected things I thought you'd be interested to hear about."

"Such as?"

He couldn't help but to blurt it out. "We found a dead body."

In a movie, there would have been crickets chirping, it was so obviously quiet.

Dad's voice was a little quieter this time. No more booming salesman. "Nick, did you say you found a—"

"Yes, we found a corpse."

"In the house?" Mom's voice was shaky.

He paused. "I need to start at the beginning."

"Please do." Dad was recovering, and he could hear the curiosity in his voice.

"First, when we went into the basement, we found a door. Do you remember the big old cabinet that used to sit against the wall, and Granny kept canned goods in it?"

"Sure. She said it was there as long as she could remember."

"Well, it's gone now. When we went down there, I thought I could see where the concrete wall had been patched. When I got closer, I could tell it looked like a door, so we scraped around it. Sure enough, it was a door. The concrete was fairly new, as if it had been sealed off recently, but the door was old."

"A door? Where would a door in the basement go?"

He grinned at the attention in his dad's voice. "It went to a tunnel."

"A tunnel? In the basement? I can't wait to see this. Where does the tunnel go?"

"I'm not sure. We didn't get all the way through it. We kinda got sidetracked when we stumbled across a corpse."

6

"You've got to be kidding." Steve Reno shook his head in disbelief. "I worked construction for over thirty years and never found anything even remotely interesting at a worksite beyond the odd Coke bottle left in the studs. I'll bet your fancy TV people never found a dead guy."

"Not that I can recall." Lisa laughed. It would have made for good television.

Del held up his hand. "What about the grow operation at the house on the river?"

"A good crop of marijuana does not compare to finding a corpse. The smell alone trumps it. And don't forget the kittens." Lisa grinned when her father and brother groaned. "Hey, they were cute."

Roxy chuckled. "You need more cats the same as you need a hole in the head."

Since moving into her own place, Lisa now had three inside cats and fed most of the strays in the neighborhood.

"I know. I was going to take them to the shelter, but the detective wouldn't let me back in the basement." She wrinkled her nose. "Not that I wanted to go back in there until it's had time to air out some more."

"They've lived there this long, I'm sure they're getting in and out somehow." Dad looked up, not quite rolling his eyes, but the effect was there.

"How long had it been there?" Del was curious. "I mean, when Nick and I went through it right after he bought it, was it there?"

"I haven't heard the time of death yet. The blood was pretty dried. I didn't see any more than I had to. What I saw wasn't pretty." A shiver went up her spine. "I had tripped on one of the cats. What if I'd tripped on the body? Ugh."

"Any idea who the guy was?" Dad shook his head. "You don't think about things like that happening around here."

"Clay didn't mention recognizing him, so he must not have been from around here. They took the body to the lab in Madisonville. I'm sure they'll ID it soon." She glanced at her dad. "Kinda scary, isn't it?"

He nodded. "The world just keeps getting crazier and crazier."

Roxy patted his shoulder as she got up to stir the jambalaya, which was teasing their noses and making their mouths water. It smelled so much better than what she had experienced, but how long until she got an appetite back?

"When will it be ready?" Dad was getting impatient.

"About ten minutes."

"Could we go ahead and eat the cobbler?" He quirked an eyebrow at his fiancée, who gave him a dirty look.

"You know the answer to that. Besides, it's better when it sits a little while." She pulled plates, bowls, and glasses out of the cupboard.

Lisa got up and started putting ice in glasses, then put the silverware and plates on the table. "Do you have napkins?" She stared imperiously at her brother.

"Who do you take me for? Martha Stewart? Paper towels are manly napkins."

She sighed as she tore off four sheets then folded them neatly, staring at her brother the whole time she worked.

"See? They are perfect."

"Back to the house, if we're not eating. What's the status, then? Will you be able to start work on it?" Contractor dad wanted to figure out the logistics.

Lisa nodded. "We'll have to wait until Clay releases it, but that's okay. I'm putting together a couple of different scenarios anyway."

"Good idea. With a hundred-year-old house..."

"Part of it is about a hundred and fifty years old."

He nodded. "I remember being in it a few times when Nick's dad, Dan, lived there. We were in high school together. It's close to where the Woodwards settled in the early 1800s, so it makes sense. A lot of the original houses burned or were hit by tornadoes, but this one must have been well-preserved. Probably built onto before it got in bad shape."

"That's what I figure. Now it has the appearance of a craftsman farmhouse, but a lot of those changes came with an addition in the early 1900s, when they added to the front."

"Nice. I wish I could get my hands on a house with so much history."

Lisa smiled at the dreamy look on her dad's face, and the frown on Roxy's.

"But you can't, because we're going on a honeymoon trip to Alaska if you recall."

He waved her off. "I know. But a guy can dream, can't he?" He winked at Lisa. "Maybe I could come over when the state police are done, and you can show me around?"

"I'd love to. If brother-dear were more mobile, I'd take him, too."

Del shook his head. "Don't worry about the invalid."

"I wasn't worried. Just being the nice, lovable sister I always am." Lisa gave him her most saccharine smile.

"The invalid may be sick."

"Clay, what are you doing here?" Lisa faced the man who had simultaneously pursued and annoyed her since primary school as he stood on the stoop of her brother's house.

"I saw your truck here, and needed to talk to you." He seemed nervous and was having difficulty looking her in the eye.

"About?" Lisa cocked her head to one side and raised her eyebrows, encouraging him to speak.

Clay glanced away and took a deep breath, then took off his hat and glared at her. "Mind if I come in?"

She backed up and opened the door wider for him to come past her. "Do you need Del?"

"Maybe. I was looking for you." He perched on the edge of a chair inside the door.

"Okay, you found me. Does this have anything to do with the house we're working on? Or attempting to work on?"

Del, Roxy, and Dad came into the room. When Clay saw Roxy, he stood up.

"Keep your seat, Clay. Can I get you some coffee? Tea?" Roxy was hostess no matter where she was.

"No, ma'am, I'm here on business."

"What's this about, Sheriff?" Dad narrowed his eyes.

He hesitated, scanning from one face to another.

"It's all right, Clay, you can talk in front of my family."

He nodded and took out his notepad. "Lisa, can you account for your whereabouts on or around June fifteenth?"

Why were her eyes so dry? Oh. She hadn't blinked. Her eyes widened at the question. "June fifteenth?" She looked at Del, Dad, and Roxy. "Am I a suspect?"

"We're calling you and Nick 'persons of interest' right now."

She couldn't help it. She laughed. He was so serious. "You've got to be kidding me." She widened her eyes at the expression on his face, then turned to her father for affirmation. "Dad?"

Her dad scooted to the edge of the sofa. "Now Clay, what's going on? Since when does finding a body constitute making the finder a suspect?"

Clay held up his hand. He didn't crack a smile. "I didn't say she was a suspect. I'm trying to get my ducks in a row before the detective from the state police weighs in."

"Had the body been there that long?"

"It's very preliminary, but it's looking like it's been there at least that long. We're still trying to get an I.D.."

Lisa sagged a little, shaking her head in disbelief. "I didn't even get close. Have you talked to Nick?"

"I have. He mentioned he and Del had gone through the house around that time."

"But it's me you're questioning?" Lisa frowned and glanced over at her brother, who was giving her the stink-eye. "Sorry, Del."

Clay flipped through a couple of pages of notes, not meeting her eyes until he found what he was searching for. "I'm getting to him. Now, can you tell me what you were doing on the fifteenth of June?"

She pulled out her phone and opened the calendar app. Her planner was in the truck, but fortunately, her Google calendar items were still viewable for June. Scrolling through, she found the week surrounding the date in question. "It was a busy week. I was in Paducah ordering bathroom fixtures for the Chase project on the fourteenth. On the fifteenth I went to Evansville shopping for flooring and tile for the Jones' renovation. Melanie was with me and we made a day of it after we found what we were looking for."

"So you haven't been far out of town any day that week?"

"No, if you don't call sixty-five miles far. I wasn't away overnight if that's what you mean." She held out her phone to show him her appointments.

He gave it a cursory glance and nodded. "I guess I don't need to tell you to stay handy."

"Is this the 'don't leave town' speech?" She was trying not to be flippant, but it made no sense. Why would she be on his radar?

"Just a friendly suggestion." He rose and made to leave. "Del, I imagine you'll be home later? I want to talk to Nick again, then I'll be back to ask you a few questions."

"Aren't you afraid we'll get together and work on getting our 'story' straight?" Del gave the word "story" air quotes. Lisa wanted to laugh, but she kept a straight face.

Clay sighed. "Del, I know it seems ridiculous, but there's a dead man, and I'm simply doing my job."

Lisa stood to see him to the door. "I'm sorry. It seems so preposterous, but I appreciate you sticking to procedure." She glanced back at Del, Dad, and Roxy. "I mean, if something had happened to one of my family members, I'd certainly want you to do everything exactly the way you are."

The sheriff gave her a half smile. "Thanks, Lisa. That means a lot to me." He waved at the rest of the family, nodded to Lisa, and went out the door.

"June fifteenth?" Nick had his calendar spread out on the tailgate of his truck. Fortunately, he kept pretty good notes. "As I've already told you, I met Del at the house on June twelfth, briefly. Around eleven, we went to the café for lunch, and I had a meeting with an HVAC guy in Eddyville at two o'clock."

"What did you do before you met Del?" Clay put his sunglasses back on to cut the glare from the white pages of the planner.

"I checked on the Eddyville project first thing, was there until time to meet Del. I was running late, and he beat me there."

"I see." Clay was busy scribbling on his notepad.

"What?"

"I see I need to get more specific when I talk to Del."

Nick sighed. This was getting them nowhere. "Listen, Sheriff, when I arrived at the house on June twelfth, Del was sitting in his truck, talking to his dad on the phone. I remember because he told me later his dad was asking him to be best man at his wedding."

Clay looked up from his notes. "So as far as you know, he hadn't been in the house yet."

"No, because I had the keys, and he didn't." That should stop this line of questioning.

"Gotcha. Of course, these old houses aren't exactly hard to get into if you try."

Nick paused to think. True. But was there any reason why Del would want to kill anyone? It was ludicrous. "When we went into the house, there were no signs of a break-in, and Del didn't know where the stairs to the basement were. I had to show him."

"Did you go back to the house for any reason over the course of the next few days?" Clay wasn't letting it go.

"No. The next time I went to the house was yesterday when I met Lisa there." He pointed to his calendar. "As you can see, I've been pretty busy this summer."

"That you have, Nick. And I assume there are folks who can corroborate these meetings?"

"I would imagine." Nick crossed his arms and stood there, waiting as Clay perused his calendar, making notes.

Clay head jerked up suddenly. "When you met Lisa yesterday, who got there first?"

Seriously? This guy thinks Lisa is a suspect? Incredible. "Actually, Lisa got there first. She was on the porch talking on the phone when I arrived, so I waited a few minutes before I joined her to tour the house."

"I see." He paused. "So Lisa had the opportunity to go into the house and be out front before you got there."

"Opportunity does not mean she had been in the house. Maybe she had been. She knew her way around except for the basement. She had keys because I had given them to Del. But I really don't think..."

"Don't worry. I don't jump to conclusions. I don't think Lisa and Del are involved, either, but I have to keep all the facts straight."

Nick nodded. "Good. When I bought the house in March, there was a large cabinet in front of where we found the door yesterday, and it was still there the first time Del and I looked at it in April, and in June when Del and I went down there to start making plans. I thought it was built-in because it was there when my grandparents lived there."

"But it wasn't there yesterday?"

"No. Which means...?"

"Which means the murder may have occurred after you went in the house in June?"

Nick pointed at him. "Or the body was already there." He frowned. But where did the cabinet go? And who had sealed off the door with plaster?

The bell on the door jingled as Lisa entered the café. Roxy's domain, the Clementville Café, wasn't just a good place to eat, it was the only place to eat that wasn't home. Unless, of course, you wanted to drive the ten miles into Marion. As it was, people drove to Clementville from all over. Roxy had started keeping a guest book when she took over the restaurant and now had a map with a pin for guests from outside Crittenden County. So far, home-folks transplanted to Hawaii and cyclists from Germany were their farthest travelers.

She scanned the dining room and didn't see Roxy or Darcy, Roxy's daughter. Eating lunch alone was not her idea of a good time, but it was part of being a single adult. She wanted to show her community that she wasn't the little redheaded, freckle-faced girl that was Steve and Carol Reno's youngest, but a businesswoman in her own right, and if she wanted to go in and order lunch by herself, then, by doggie, she would.

Just as she started looking for an empty booth, her phone buzzed.

"Sandwiches upstairs. And pie. Come on up."

Crisis averted. Until she glanced up to see a familiar face.

"Hey there, Lisa. How's your daddy doin'?"

Mr. Dixon was her old elementary school principal. He was busy stuffing bills in his wallet, so he had his hands full, thank goodness. His distracted expression gave her the impression that he'd like to pat her on the head as he did when she was in second grade.

"He's doing great, Mr. Dixon." She tried to smile and not get the quivery feeling you always get when faced with someone in your past that instilled a little fear, even when you hadn't done anything.

"Tell him I said hello. What are you up to these days? Are you still in school?"

That did it. She was going to have to up her game in the makeup and wardrobe department. Working for her dad and Del, she had relaxed her "look" and wore what was comfortable on a job site—jeans, boots, and a long-sleeved shirt.

Apparently, her ensemble did not age her up.

"No, Mr. Dixon, I'm working with my brother, Del, in Dad's construction company. He's semi-retired now. I got my degree in interior design a few years ago."

He had the grace to feign surprise. "Did you, now? Well, I'll be. You're making me feel old, young lady."

They laughed and as he turned, he did it. He didn't shake her hand. He did the unthinkable.

He patted her on the head.

7

Lisa was red-faced from much more than the walk up the stairs to Roxy's loft above the café.

"Are you all right?" Roxy looked at her strangely.

She pulled herself together and shook her head. "I'm fine." She arched a brow. "I ran into someone who's forgotten I'm not in second grade."

"Remember this when you're fifty. You'll be glad people think you're forty!"

"Maybe. Right now, it's hard to break out of the idea of 'she's just Steve and Carol's little girl' to be considered an adult who owns a business in the community. You know?"

Darcy brought plates and napkins to the table. "One of the downsides of working for your parents. I get it all the time."

Lisa widened her eyes and said emphatically. "He had the gall to ask if I was still in school."

Roxy and Darcy laughed, and she groaned. "You're right. Pushing thirty and looking twenty might not be so bad, after all."

Roxy squeezed her hand on the table and twisted her lips in a smile. "I'm sorry I laughed, but you have to admit, it's pretty funny."

"Plus, he can't see worth a hoot." Darcy shook her head and grinned. "He's due for cataract surgery in the next few months, so I've practically been reading the menu for him."

"Bless his heart. I guess I need to remember it's not all about me." She smiled.

"No, today it's all about me!" Roxy gave the girls a wink. "You know I'm kidding, right?"

Lisa and Darcy looked at one another and laughed. Darcy sighed. "Well, it is *your day* we're talking about."

Lisa pulled out her notebook designated "Dad and Roxy Get Married" and flipped to a tab labeled "floral."

"The flowers will be ready to pick up on the eighteenth." Lisa grinned at her soon-to-be stepmother, Roxy, and stepsister, Darcy. "I can't wait to try putting the bouquets together."

"Are you sure you don't want to order them? I'm sure Teena would be glad to do it, even on short notice." Roxy was beginning to get nervous, Lisa could tell. Darcy winked at Lisa before addressing her mother. "Mom, we can do this." Darcy reached for her mother's hand. "Lisa is artistic, and I'm organized. There's nothing we can't do to make this a beautiful wedding."

"I know. I wanted a simple ceremony, but it seems to have morphed into something I didn't imagine." Roxy shook her head but smiled at the two girls.

"I always wanted a sister, you know. Del left something to be desired when I wanted him to play with me. Somehow my Barbie dolls always ended up beheaded or in a war-scene instead of going on the perfect date." Lisa laughed.

Darcy grinned. "I'm sure. Well, I didn't have anybody, so my Barbie dolls did whatever I told them to do." She sighed as she considered Lisa. "I always wanted a sister, too. And now I have one."

"What's really cool is I'm not only getting a sister but a niece and nephew, too." Lisa raised her shoulders in an excited shrug. "Did you get those pictures back yet?"

Darcy got her phone out and flipped through until she found the site of the photographer who had taken the twins' summer portraits. "Here they are. They turned out so good. They'll be three in November, but a trip to the beach warranted pictures."

"Most definitely. I'm so glad you got to go." Lisa oohed and aahed over the toddlers' adorable images in the photographs.

"June and Mike have been so good to us. I know it's hard. Justin was their only child, and now their grandchildren live so far away. I'm glad we went at Christmas."

Darcy nodded as she took the phone from Lisa and glanced through a few images.

Roxy smiled. "They're good in-laws."

"The best." Darcy gave her mother a misty smile. "Now, back to you, Mother dear."

"I have my dress and my shoes, the tabernacle is booked and the hall is rented."

"What hall? We're having the reception on the church grounds." Lisa arched an eyebrow at her.

"Exactly. How's that for saving big bucks. We'll have to close, but most everyone will be at the wedding anyway." She laughed. "We're saving money on a venue, and losing money by feeding everybody."

"True, but it's the wedding of the year, you know." Lisa grinned. "It was great of the Hurricane Camp board to let you and Dad use the tabernacle for the wedding."

"Your dad has put a lot of work into the property, and we're going to make a donation to the camp fund to keep the summer camp going. It's a special place, you know. Your mom and I got to be good friends there when we were kids."

"She told me. Did you know Dad then?"

"Of course I did. Every year, the boys somehow gained access to the girls' cabin and trashed it. He was the ringleader, usually, but our last year there, while we were in middle school, he tipped your mom off and we caught them. I think he had a crush on her even then." Roxy grinned and took a deep breath and looked from her daughter to her soon-to-be stepdaughter. "I can't believe how time has changed things." She chuckled as she wiped a tear from her eye. "But I know one thing: only in a town the size of Clementville will a wedding between a couple in their fifties be the 'wedding of the year.'"

"This is ridiculous. You know I didn't have anything to do with this." Del was annoyed, and he didn't mind if Clay knew it.

The sheriff ran his hand through his hair and leaned back on the sofa across from Del and his thigh-high leg brace in the recliner. "I have to do this, Del, and you know it. The KSP detective will be on the scene tomorrow, and I want to have my ducks in a row. If you cooperate now, maybe you won't have to deal with them."

Del took a deep breath. His leg hurt. The ache had been there all day, but now it was beginning to yell at him. He hadn't wanted to say anything, but the pain pill he had taken a few hours ago was wearing off and he'd been on his feet more in the last few days than he had since the accident. He closed his eyes and tried to calm himself before he said something that made things worse.

"Okay. Sorry. Just not great timing, you know?"

"I know. Let's go over this again." Clay glanced down at his notepad at the scribbles he had made when he talked to Nick and Lisa. "Nick says the first time you allegedly inspected the house..."

"No 'allegedly' to it, Clay, it was the first time."

"The first time you allegedly inspected the house, in March," Clay scrutinized him pointedly, "you were there ahead of him. Is there anyone you may have passed along the way that could corroborate your timeline?"

Del snorted. "You saw where the place was. Nobody lives out there except some Amish families and a few coyotes and deer."

"Okay, that's a start. Did you pass any buggies or people walking along the road?" Clay leaned forward.

Del closed his eyes, thinking. Had he seen anyone? "You know how those roads are, Clay. Passing buggies and kids walking down the road are an everyday occurrence."

"Think, Del."

"I am thinking." He paused, brows furrowed in concentration. "I may have passed a buggy, but I don't know who it would have been." He looked up at Clay and shrugged his shoulders. "Once I get around a buggy, I don't usually gawk back to see if it's someone I know."

"I understand. But if you did pass a buggy, it would be a place to start. I could question the folks that live along the road." Clay made a note.

"Wait a minute."

"You think of something?" Clay was at attention.

"I passed another car at the end of the road. It was stopped. I rolled my window down and asked if they needed help, but they said they were trying to get a signal for their GPS."

"Anybody you know?"

Del shook his head. "No. Never saw them before."

"Did you get a look at the license plate?"

Del grinned. "When you live around here and see a strange car, you always check out the license plate to see if they're foreigners." Meaning "not from around here" rather than actual residents of a foreign country. "They had Illinois plates, which didn't really mean much since we were a mile from the ferry crossing to Illinois."

"Yeah, could be anybody." Clay wrote it down.

"With Riverfront Park down the road, there's more traffic than there used to be, especially on a pretty day."

Clay considered that thoughtfully. "Good point."

8

Lisa had an appointment to meet Nick at the job site, so she'd stopped by the office on her dad's property to pick up the preliminary plans. She wished Del could be there. She didn't feel completely comfortable meeting with Nick alone, and she knew it was silly. It was as if she had turned right back into the awkward teenager that had a crush on him instead of the accomplished, savvy designer she had become. Maybe it was an overstatement, but she preferred to think she presented a polished exterior, anyway.

She was putting on lip gloss before getting out of her truck when she saw her dad come out the side door of the house, wearing his work clothes. What was he up to? The heart attack that almost got him at Christmas had propelled him into both retirement and a romance, and he promised he wouldn't interfere with the business until after his and Roxy's honeymoon. The doctor had suggested he retire completely, but he would only agree to semi-retirement.

"Hey, Dad. Whatcha doin'?" She grabbed her tote and slammed the truck door as he approached her.

He kissed her on the cheek and grinned. "I thought I'd drive over to the worksite. You look awful nice this morning."

She gave him a small curtsy. "Why thank you, kind sir. I doubt you can get in. The KSP detectives were supposed to be there this morning. We still don't know when it will be released." She arched an eyebrow at him. "Besides, aren't you supposed to be meeting the pastor with

Roxy this morning? Pre-marital counseling, I believe?" A giggle escaped her lips and she clapped her hand over her mouth.

His face flushed. "Yeah, but it's not for a couple of hours. I wanted to find something to do to get my mind off it." He lifted his hands into the air. "How can a young pup like Pastor Aaron tell an old guy like me about life? He's young enough to be my kid."

She laughed out loud. "I know. I thought it was pretty funny, too." She slipped her hand around her dad's waist and hugged him. "But he loves you guys, and it's part of his wedding package, so you may as well take it with love and a grain of salt."

"Yeah, I will, for Roxy's sake. I don't want to embarrass her."

"Or make her change her mind." She poked him in the ribs.

"Exactly." He squeezed her and then let go, then put his hands in his pockets. "What do you have going on today?"

She unlocked the office door and went in, Dad following. "You're in luck. I'm meeting Nick at the house if you want to come along. Thought I'd sketch out some of the ideas we talked about. Since we can't get in the house, there's no reason we can't put plans to paper and be ready when the time comes to do the demo."

He took a seat and nodded as he studied the large sheet of paper on her desk. "Lots of changes, huh?"

"Dad, you would love it. Or hate it. There will be lots of engineering to consider with this project to get the open floor plan."

Dad glanced at her over the top of his glasses. Classic Dad. Even with bifocals, he defaulted to his natural vision to make his point. "You sure you and Del can handle this?" He shook his head and looked back down at the plans. "His accident came out of nowhere."

She paused, thinking. "I wonder if I could let him take over some of the bookkeeping while he's laid up."

He gave her a sidelong glance. "Are you sure?"

"After that one snafu, he pays a lot more attention to the numbers.

It might be good for him to be able to work on both sides of the business. With Nick's help, I'm doing the contractor work, so it would only be fair."

He shifted in his seat. It was driving him crazy not to be in charge. "I guess so. Keep an eye on it, though."

Lisa's drafting table sat next to a window facing south for the best light in winter. In summer, she loved it because the trees on the perimeter shaded her, but still gave her plenty of light. Seasonal Affective Disorder is real, and the sunlight helped. She pulled her notes and laptop from her tote. "See, here's a rough draft."

He pointed to one of the walls on the plan. "Looks like an addition, but is it?"

"Pretty sure it is. The windows appear to be newer and less substantial."

He adjusted his glasses and inspected it closely. "You might be able to get away with widening the casements and keeping the headers smaller."

"Maybe." She closed her notebook and stared at him, arms akimbo. "Dad. You're not on this project, remember?"

He chuckled. "Yeah, but you can't blame me for being interested in this one. It's a great house."

"It is. When I first saw it, I wanted to kill Del for getting us into it, but it's growing on me." Now she had to get up the nerve to go back into the house.

"So it's for Nick Woodward, huh?" He arched an eyebrow at her. "Seems to me I remember hearing his name from more than Del." He laughed at her reddening face. "I like Nick. I hear he's a good worker."

Dad may be retired, but it didn't stop him from automatically heading to the driver's side of the truck. Some battles weren't worth fighting, so Lisa hid her grin and rode shotgun.

She bounced a little when they hit a pothole on the county road. "Here's the drive, on the left."

The view of the grand old house made her smile every time she drove in, and with Dad driving, she was able to appreciate it on a different level. Whoever did the front addition had done an excellent job of integrating the older structure in the back.

"Did you know there was once a whole community out here?" Dad put the truck in gear and unbuckled his seatbelt. "There was a Woodward back in the early 1800s who intended to build a town here, and call it 'Salinaville' after his wife, Salina Crofton Woodward."

"What happened? I mean, there are a few houses within a five-mile radius, and there's an old store building where we turned off, but I'm guessing his dream wasn't realized."

He shook his head. "He was killed in a sawmill accident when he was forty years old. There used to be a house right on the river that he built."

"Wow."

They exited the truck and stood, studying the front elevation of the house. "I've been out here, but it's been a long time. I'd say the gutters, what's left of them, are shot."

Lisa wasn't ready to leave the history lesson. "So, does this house have any ties to the original Woodwards?"

He nodded. "His son built the original structure here, and then his grandson built the front."

Lisa turned when she heard a truck arriving. Nick. The last thing she wanted was for her crazy redhead complexion to go crazy red with her dad there.

Nick raked his hair back, and Lisa wanted to laugh. Apparently, he hadn't gotten his mop of hair completely under control. When they were in college he'd been known for his frequent haircuts. But even then, he always seemed to have hair in his face.

Dad put his hand out. "How are you, Nick?"

"I'm good. It's been a while, sir."

"It has. I haven't seen you since you worked under Jim White."

Nick shook his hand. "He was good. Taught me everything I know about construction."

"Great guy. I worked with him on a few projects. I subbed his concrete guys a few times when mine was busy, and we did mission trips together."

"He mentioned you. When he found out Del and I were buddies, I think it made him think a little more highly of me than he probably should."

"No, Jim was a good judge of character. Miss him."

"Me, too. His stroke came out of nowhere."

Dad shook his head. "Certainly made me take stock."

Lisa shot a glance at her dad and thought about his own glimpse of mortality.

Seeming to shake off maudlin thoughts, Dad grinned at Nick and then squinted up at the house. "I'm looking forward to seeing the inside of this place again."

Nick nodded. "You and Dad went to school together, didn't you?"

"We did. Since we both lived out this way, we partnered up on a few FFA projects together. How's Dan doing?"

"He's good. Getting ready to retire from the insurance business."

"I was approached about selling insurance when I was fresh out of college, but a tool belt fits me better than a suit and tie, so I went my own way. Dan was always a good salesman, though. He won all the impromptu speech competitions we entered."

"That's my dad. He can talk, that's for sure." Nick's face tightened a bit as he spoke of his father. Lisa wondered.

Dad grinned at Nick with understanding. She was glad when he changed the subject.

"Lisa tells me Clay's got it marked off as a crime scene."

"I got the go-ahead from the KSP last night, so we're clear to go in, except for the basement." He mounted the steps.

Lisa stopped them with a hand on Nick's arm. "So what did they tell you?"

He turned to her. "Sorry, I should have called you when I found out. I'm sure you're curious."

Hands on her hips, she glared. "A little. It's not every day you stumble upon a dead body."

"True." He laughed and looked down at her. Did he have a little glint in his eye? She was imagining things. Had to be. "They've estimated the time of death early April."

"Wasn't that about the time you and Del came out here?" She felt the blood drain from her face, and the mere thought of them stumbling on a freshly-dead corpse, or even worse, a murderer, almost made her sick.

"We did. No sign of anything out of the ordinary then. The cabinet was still there when we went in April, and again in June." He shook his head in sympathy. "Anyway, they went all the way through the tunnel."

"And?" She held out her hands, waiting for his answer.

"It went all the way to the river. Well, almost. It went to a cellar about fifty yards from the riverbank."

"Dad, you don't think?" Lisa tilted her head oddly and scrutinized her dad.

"What?" Nick was curious. "Is there something about it I need to know?"

Steve shifted his jaw and narrowed his eyes. "Could we drive out there and see where it comes up?"

Lisa seemed excited. "Dad was telling me about the connection between this house and a house that used to be right on the river. Have you ever heard of Salinaville or the Crofton family?"

Nick nodded. "Sure. One of my great-grandmothers—I can't remember how far back—was Salina Crofton Woodward. Do you think the cellar they found was part of the original Woodward house?"

"Dan and I used to go out there and build fires in the old fireplace when we were kids. Great place to cook up some fish. I don't remember a cellar opening."

Nick frowned. "Yeah, I know my great-grandparents lived there until they died, then it burned a few years later. I went out there a few times, but I never saw anything like that, either."

"You may have another mystery on your hands besides the dead body." Steve grinned. "You kids may have to play Scooby-Doo before it's all over."

Nick snorted. "Yeah, we'll solve mysteries between moving walls and shoring up foundations." He glanced down at Lisa with concern. "Are you sure you want to go in there?"

She nodded. "We need to if we can." She hesitated. "Has it aired out any?"

"It's much better. They gave me the name of a cleaning service that takes care of these things, and they came out yesterday for an estimate and will come back to clean when it's been cleared. Until then, they left some strong deodorizer pouches in the basement and house."

She took a deep breath. "All right then, let's get in the house and get Dad to the other site because he's got an appointment in a few hours." Lisa grinned at her dad's sheepish demeanor. She took charge and bounced up the front steps, neatly side-stepping the hole she had made previously. "Watch the soft spot."

"Hon, that's not a soft spot. That's a hole. About size six and a half, if you ask me." Steve looked at his daughter, eyebrows raised.

"She found that one the other day." Nick held up his hands and laughed at her reddening face. "I have to say, she did fall through the floor gracefully."

"Good to know those ballet lessons were worth something."

"Very funny."

Nick unlocked the front door and held it open for his "guests." Lisa went in slowly, at first, sniffing the air. "Oh, this is much better." She swept in as if she owned the place. Since she was the contractor, in a sense, she did. For a while, anyway.

"Look at this, Dad. It has so much potential." She did a little twirl in front of the foyer mirror that was cloudy with age.

Nick noticed that as she gazed around, she sighed a little. There were some houses like that, he supposed. Houses that felt good as soon as you walked in. Musty smells and the memory of a corpse in the tunnel below notwithstanding.

"As long as it doesn't break me." Nick stuffed his hands in his pockets and looked around, trying to see it through her eyes.

Lisa shook her head with confidence. "It won't. You'll be surprised how much difference a good clean-up will make."

Steve nodded. "She's right. Get the demo crew in to clean it up first, then take stock again. The floors in here feel sound, and the staircase looks good and straight." He walked over to the wide doorway into the front parlor and pulled out the pocket door.

"I think we could use a squirt of WD-40 on the mechanism." Nick was amazed at the quality of craftsmanship when the oak door slid into view on its tracks, but the screeching sound made him wince.

"See?" Lisa pointed to the door. "This is what's hiding underneath the surface." She took a deep breath and then sneezed.

"Bless you."

"Thank you." She reached for a tissue in her jeans pocket and came up empty.

Nick pulled one out and handed it to her. "Here you go."

"My hero." She grinned. "Anyway, it's stuff like those doors that make renovation and restoration so much fun." She turned to her dad. "Do you remember when we went to the Cupple's House on the campus of St. Louis University?"

"There was no going back for you after that." Steve chuckled. "We went up for a Cardinals game when she was in middle school and took a few side trips to the zoo and some other places. It was the house that made her want to go into restoration."

"I've been there."

"You have?" Lisa gaped at him incredulously. "And you still want to build new houses?"

"Have you seen any of my houses?" He tilted his head curiously.

"On the outside." She shrugged. "They're very nice but very new."

"I like to take modern technology and methods and marry them to old-fashioned craftsmanship."

"Makes sense. I mean, this was new tech once upon a time." Steve nodded.

"Exactly. You can ask Del. I'm a house nerd , too."

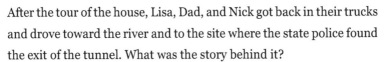

After the tour of the house, Lisa, Dad, and Nick got back in their trucks and drove toward the river and to the site where the state police found the exit of the tunnel. What was the story behind it?

And furthermore, what was the story behind Nick and this previously unknown old house geekdom?

Sitting in the truck beside her dad, Lisa was quiet.

Having come through school as a self-proclaimed introvert with a first name straight out of the sixties (thanks, Mom), she had prided herself on nurturing hobbies and interests not considered "cool" to the unwashed herd. Who wanted to be part of that group anyway?

Her love of creating floor plans, her collection of house plan books, her early attempts at creating decorating storyboards were all a result of that first trip to St. Louis. She had helped her dad all her life, but it was seeing a particular 1890 historic mansion in St. Louis that made her consider every other old house differently.

And meeting Nick Woodward when she was twenty made her behold every other man differently.

"What'cha thinkin' about, sweetie?" Dad glanced over at her from the driver's seat.

The last thing she was going to tell her father, Steve Reno, was that she was still crushing on Nick Woodward. This was a man who had been married, for goodness sake, and was a widower. It was almost as if he had lived a whole adult life, and she was recreating the movie, *Failure to Launch*.

"Just thinking about the house."

"Lots to think about. I hope you get Sonny Wilkins out to look at where you want to put in the support for the wall you want to take out. He's the best construction engineer I know."

She glared over at him with a withering glance, she hoped. "Dad, you know we will. He's on the top of the list." *Retire, already, Dad?* She wouldn't dare say it out loud, but it was screaming in her head.

"I know. Has he thought about trying to get it on the National Register of Historic Places?"

He seemed concerned. She would be, too, if Nick decided to go that route. While it had its perks, tax-wise, it limited what you could do to a house and stay within their guidelines.

"I hope not."

"I do too. A house like this needs to be lived in. Is Nick going to live in it, or sell it?"

Surely he wouldn't sell it outside of his family. Surely.

"I'm not sure. We really haven't talked about it."

"Hm. I'd say you two were communicating pretty well out there. I mean, you did find a body together."

She shivered. "I'd rather not think about that part if you don't mind."

He laughed and pointed down the side road they had turned on. "The old house place was right up here. There's the old fireplace. I remember it smoked like crazy. The chimney was probably completely blocked, but we didn't care."

"That sounds safe."

"Yeah. Amazing how we survived childhood and young-adulthood back then." He winked at her as he put the truck in gear.

"You're invincible, Dad." She leaned over and kissed his cheek before getting out of the truck.

9

Pulling up beside Steve's truck, Nick observed as father and daughter walked around and met in front of the vehicle. Both Lisa and her dad stood facing the crumbling chimney of the old Woodward homestead, arms crossed in front of them. Except for the height and build difference, they were a pair. Same red hair, although Steve's was peppered with white, and same stance. Feet spread apart confidently, arms crossed, back straight.

He was smiling as he came around to them.

"What?" Lisa scrutinized him skeptically.

"Nothing." Someday he would tell her his thoughts, but not today.

"So this is where the tunnel comes out?"

"Yes ma'am."

He strode over toward the chimney and veered a little left when he got closer. "You can see where the indention of the old rock pillars used to be that held up the house." There were still several large stones lying about, too heavy for anyone to carry off, but they were scattered as if by a small child throwing rocks in a driveway.

"No concrete foundations back then." Steve shook his head.

Nick laughed. "Nothing but cold air and animals trying to stay warm under the house."

"I love old houses, but animals under the house would be the limit for me." Lisa shuddered.

"Me, too. That's the beauty of combining the old and the new." He picked his way a little further. "Here's where the back porch used to be, I think."

The cellar doors were right there, next to a pile of stones. The footprints around the low structure denoted the traffic that had been through both recently, and not-so-recently.

Steve examined it closely. "Somebody has replaced these doors." He looked up at them.

"This is fairly new lumber. I don't remember any of this from before."

"Maybe the old doors were under some of the big rocks. Last time I was here, the only thing I remember is the chimney. The detective told me I might want to get a game camera or something out here." Nick surveyed the area, wondering where he could mount surveillance equipment that wouldn't be spotted immediately.

"Good idea. Is this property yours, too?"

He nodded slowly. "It's part of the original farm. None of the family wanted it, so I bought them out."

"Do you plan to live here?" Lisa gazed up at him. Did she know how pretty she was?

Did he? He didn't want it to go out of the family, but was he ready to pull up stakes and move out here?

Lisa watched her dad and Nick pull open the cellar doors and reveal the wooden steps going down into the dark hole in the ground. "When was the old house built?" She wasn't sure how much she could trust those steps.

"From what Gran told me, the original log house was built around 1830, and then they built on when the fourth child came." He took a step down. "Looks like the steps were repaired a while back."

"No way are these nearly two hundred-year-old planks." Dad bounced on the top step

Lisa raised an eyebrow as she tried it out. "Especially considering it's treated lumber."

Nick took the lead with his Maglite flashlight, with Lisa in the middle and Dad behind. She felt very safe. Would there come a time when her diminutive stature didn't make all her menfolk think she had to be protected? Maybe she shouldn't complain, but simply be glad they cared. And since when did Nick Woodward fit into the role of "her menfolk"?

"Careful, there's a tree root up ahead." Nick stepped over it, then shone his light on it for Lisa.

She stopped and put her hands on her hips.

"Hey, I didn't want you to trip." He winked at her as she huffed.

They hadn't gone far when she began to hear the faint sound of mewling. The cat and kittens had to be up ahead. Had they really gone as far as the tunnel on the other side?

"What was that?" Dad's hearing wasn't the best, but he heard it, too.

Lisa answered him. "Probably that poor cat and kittens."

"Great. You need to get them out of here, Nick. They'll be getting into the house if you're not careful." Dad gave her a pointed look, even as he spoke to Nick.

Lisa spoke up. "I'll get them out, Dad. I couldn't the other day because it was a crime scene."

"That's about the lamest excuse for not getting rid of cats I've ever heard." Dad laughed out loud, Nick joining him as they plotted against her and her love of cats. Men.

"I'll take them to the animal shelter in the next few days. Don't worry. I could take them home..."

"Don't you think three cats are enough?" Dad shook his head and shone his little flashlight toward her. "Face it, daughter, you're well on your way to becoming the crazy cat lady."

"Nice." Why did her family think it was okay to tease her about her cats and her marital status? Or lack thereof. Del wasn't married, either, but nobody minded. She thought about the classic sitcom, *The Beverly Hillbillies*, and wondered how Elly May Clampett felt when her family thought she was an old maid at seventeen?

"Unless we want to walk another half mile, I'd suggest we turn back. We haven't gotten to the other tunnel yet, but they've taped it off and asked me to stay out of it until they have time to check it out more closely." Nick stopped, shining his light around what appeared to be yet another larger opening in the cave. "Whoever dug this tunnel took advantage of the naturally occurring caves."

"This one's almost as big as Cave-In-Rock." Lisa surveyed the area as the two men slowly illuminated the underground cavern. "We should come back with lanterns sometime."

"I'd be game for that." Nick grinned at Lisa.

Dad stood, looking around. "This is something else. I'll leave the exploring to you two. It's a shame Del's on crutches."

"Yeah, he loves caves." Lisa nodded and smiled warmly.

As Nick took the flashlight beam around one more time, slowly, he stopped at a pile of what appeared to be rubble.

"What do you see?" Lisa followed the beam, and then Nick, as he started toward it.

"Don't touch anything, just in case."

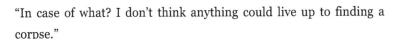

"In case of what? I don't think anything could live up to finding a corpse."

Lisa shook her head and followed him over to the pile.

Nick picked up what resembled a broom handle lying on the ground and poked at the canvas. Nothing. He pushed the tip of the stick under the edge of the cloth and pushed it away. "This is interesting."

Lisa crept up behind him and peered over his shoulder as best she could. "What is it?"

He turned to her and grinned. "Looks like a pile of junk to me."

"Good." She felt her breath whoosh out of her. She had been holding it since they came down the dark staircase.

Dad shone his larger flashlight on the pile of objects, not touching anything. "This stuff has been here for a long time."

10

Steve left them when they reconnoitered at the office, and silence held them for a moment. *Does she feel as uncomfortable as I do?*

"Um—"

"—Okay—"

They both started together, and then glanced at one another and laughed. She had a difficult time meeting his eyes. Yes, she felt it.

"You first." Nick stuffed his hands in his pockets and shrugged. He was interested in what she had to say. Very interested. Watching the light glance off her auburn hair and the expressions changing with each moment, it seemed, it was as if he was seeing her for the first time.

"Okay. Here's what I've got so far. I'm open to suggestions." She spread out the drawings, pointing out this and that feature.

"This looks good." The idea of opening the floor plan, yet keeping the integrity of the separate rooms appealed to him. "There are good sight lines, but it still has the feel of an old house."

"I thought so. I didn't want it to look like a brand-new house on the inside." She glanced up at him with a smile. "I want it to appear as if your grandmother could function in the space."

"You've got the right idea." He pointed to a section on the floor plan. "What about this? Is it load bearing?"

She shrugged her shoulders. "I'm not sure. Dad and I were talking about it before we met you at the house. If it is, then we'll need to get an engineer in to assess it. If not, we can either take it out completely or widen the casement." She twisted her lips."What do you think?"

He pondered. It was the wall between the kitchen and dining room. "I'm torn. Part of me thinks opening it up would be more practical. Another part of me would love to see a stunning dining room with a huge turkey on a platter and about twelve people around the table." He laughed and was surprised to see her gazing at him.

"I'll get some drawings of both ideas."

"You see it, don't you?" He tilted his head as if by doing so he could see her inner thoughts better. It didn't, but it brought out a smile, which was enough, for now.

"I do." She reddened slightly. "I'll get to work on this. Since we can't do any demo yet, we can have plans ready when Clay gives us permission to re-enter."

"I'm going out there when I leave here. Want to go back over, since we were a little rushed earlier?" He lifted his eyebrows in question.

She hesitated, which reminded Nick that while Lisa came across as self-assured now, she still had an indecisive introvert inside of her. "I should..."

"Go with me?" He grinned at her.

"I was going to say I should work on these drawings." She shook her head.

"Come on. You can do it later. I want to check out the wall again, and we may as well do it together." He shrugged again. "Besides, I think Clay likes you better than he does me."

"Why do you say that?"

"Oh, guys pick up on these things."

_____

Maybe Nick was right. Clay did seem to have a burr under his saddle when they walked up to him together. Men. The guy who spent their elementary years tugging her ponytail and calling her "Freckles" had the gall to act like a jealous person?

"Hey, Clay." She raised her hand in greeting when she saw the young sheriff come out on the porch.

"Hey, Lisa. Nick." He checked the clipboard in his hand, then walked down the steps to meet them. "What're y'all up to today?"

Nick reached out and shook his hand. "Just checking to see how much longer until we can get into the rest of the house."

"I'd estimate a week or more."

"Really?" Lisa glanced at Nick, and then back at Clay. "Have they identified the body yet?"

Clay shook his head. "You know I can't talk about an active investigation."

She closed her eyes and counted to ten. "Sorry. I haven't gotten my TV-cop-show training certificate in the mail yet."

The glare he shot her way sobered her immediately. "Cute. Detective Reed is in there now with a forensics team."

"In the tunnel?" Nick raised his eyebrows in question.

Clay nodded. "They're starting where the victim was found, then widening out from there. I think they're in the process of investigating the tunnel. That's all I can say, and I wouldn't say that much except you've been in the tunnel, so you know about it already."

She wanted to laugh at his serious demeanor, but she held it together. "I appreciate it, Clay. I was wondering about the cat and kittens we found."

A stout figure came out the front door with a pet transport carrier. "Somebody asking about mama cat and her entourage?" Detective Glen Reed chuckled as he set the plastic and wire carrier down at Lisa's feet. "Here's mama, but she's hidden her babies well."

She knelt at the carrier and opened the wire door. The cat came out and went straight into her arms, purring her little heart out. "We can't take her away from her babies, can we?" She looked up at the men standing over her and the cat before the feline decided to sink her claws in Lisa's shoulder before shooting out of her arms and back into the house. "Ouch."

The detective laughed. "I don't think she wants to be rescued."

"She's just worried about her kittens."

"I'll leave the carrier in the house. I caught a glimpse of one of the kittens yesterday. They were definitely born after the body was left there." Detective Reed waved off Clay when he would have interrupted. "Aw, Clay, don't worry about me spilling info. Nick here has a right to know since it's his house, and Lisa is working for him."

"But they're still..." The local lawman paused, looking from the detective to Lisa and Nick.

"Suspects?" Glen gave Clay a withering glare. "Seriously? What we've found down there points every way except to Nick, Lisa, or Del. This is bigger than all of us." Clay shook his head and walked over to where his deputies were conferring with the forensics team.

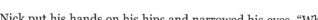

Nick put his hands on his hips and narrowed his eyes. "What do you mean, 'bigger than all of us'?"

He was stunned. But then he had been stunned when he stumbled over a corpse in his basement, so it was par for the course lately.

"I mean we've found evidence of criminal activity down there going back several years." The detective looked at him with narrowed eyes. "Your family owned this property years ago, didn't they?"

Were they accusing Grandma and Grandpa of wrongdoing? No way. "They did, but it's been out of the family for the last ten years."

"Oh, I know. It seems there was more than one operation going on over the years." Detective Reed chuckled. "Considering the artifacts and evidence we've found, through the years the series of tunnels and cellars were used for a variety of enterprises from the time this area was settled."

Nick felt, rather than saw, Lisa's eyes flash to him. She spoke up. "Enterprises?"

"It's early yet, but it appears that the most recent issue involved either a counterfeiting or money-laundering operation. Not too far down from where you came across the body..."

"Have you identified it yet?" Nick interrupted.

"No, it'll take more time due to the rate of decomposition."

Lisa paled. "Ugh."

"Yeah, it wasn't pretty. Anyway, as I was saying, we could tell by the tracks left on the dirt floor that they'd had heavy equipment moved out." He reached into his pocket and pulled out a ten-dollar bill safely ensconced in a plastic evidence bag. "But we also found this. As good as they were, it looks like they got in a hurry and missed this one."

Nick took the bag from him. He examined it closely, unable to distinguish any errors. "Is it real?"

The detective grinned. "Nope. Phony as a three-dollar bill, pun intended."

He shook his head. "It's pretty convincing."

"Very, unless you've been trained to spot counterfeit currency."

Nick handed back the phony bill and stuffed his hands in his pockets. "When can we have full access to the house?"

Reed glanced at the front door, where Clay was still talking to one of his deputies. "I wouldn't have a problem with you having the run of the place now, but the sheriff wants to do a little more digging, and with the currency we found, that brings in the FBI." He looked from one to the other and motioned for Clay to come over. When he did, the detective addressed him. "Clay, what say we let these folks get in the house to do some measuring and take a few pictures?"

"We don't need in the basement, today, just the main floor and the upstairs." Nick was trying to be agreeable, but it was getting difficult. He felt he was fighting Clay every step of the way.

Clay took a deep breath and looked from Nick to Lisa, and then to Detective Reed. "Fine, since you've been in there once already. But no demolition until the property is released from the investigation."

Nick held his hands up. "No problem. I want to inspect a few things we're thinking about changing, mainly so Lisa can make plans and order supplies while we're waiting."

"Okay. You'll need to clear it with me any time you want in." Clay squinted at Nick with a challenge in his stance.

Nick thought he heard a stifled snort next to him, from Lisa, but he squashed the chuckle threatening to escape and put on his most impassive face. "You're the boss." He glanced at Lisa, seeing the humor in her eyes, and wondered again why he hadn't noticed her years ago.

"What do you mean, the project's on hold?" Del's voice rose in frustration.

Lisa put her portfolio down on her desk.

"I mean, until the authorities get through the tunnel and identify the body we found, we're out of a job. Clay's still running the investigation. The state police would have released it already, but Clay and the FBI are still poking around in the tunnel."

"Great." Del's sigh came through the phone loud and clear.

"Don't worry about it. It will give us more time to get things the way we—I mean he—wants it." Lisa felt the heat creep up her neck. Where did the Freudian slip come from?

"This was our big project for the summer, sis. What will we do now it's off the table?"

She thought a moment. "I'm still doing design boards for Nick, and

I can start putting products together and studying the engineering. Beyond that, I've got a couple of non-construction design projects I've kept in my back pocket for a few months. I can knock those out while we wait for Nick's house to be released. I need to get Mel's nursery project done soon, anyway."

"Sounds like you've thought this through. Dad will be proud of you." Del chuckled. "Like he wouldn't be anyway."

"Well, when you're the favorite, what can you say?"

"Yeah, well..."

"I need to go, Del. I've got the measurements we took at the house today, and I need to get them down on the spreadsheet while they're still fresh. I'll keep you posted." She cradled the phone on her shoulder and opened the folder holding her numbers. "How are you feeling?" It was an afterthought, but at least she asked.

"I'm okay. Hey, can you take me to physical therapy on Monday?" He paused. "I hate to ask, but with Dad tied up and me not able to drive..."

"Sure I can. What time?"

He groaned audibly. "Eight thirty. I know. It's early for a trip to Paducah, but I hope they can transfer me down to Marion after the first visit."

"I hope so. That would be a lot more doable."

"Thanks, sis. Hey, get busy. You've got the business in your hands these days."

"I know." She sighed. "We'll be okay, and Dad will be home in a little over a month."

11

Lisa blinked back tears as she watched her dad and Roxy walk together down the aisle of the Hurricane Tabernacle. She still couldn't believe her dad was getting married.

She loved Roxy. Really, she did. She didn't try to take the place of her mother, but she was there for her, and then there was the bonus of a sister, niece, and nephew. There was no downside. For two years, Dad had been alone after Mom died, and they thought it would always be that way.

But last Christmas had more magic than Santa Claus. It was a miracle that began in Heaven and manifested on Earth when a heart attack and a toddler's head bump coincided and two lonely people had their eyes opened.

Her heart gladdened as she listened to the soft music playing from a violin and guitar off to the side. Dad had told her that her playing would be the best music a father could ask for, but he knew two things: she wouldn't be able to focus on the wedding, *and* the piano at the outdoor tabernacle was consistently out of tune.

She had to wonder about her own future wedding—would she remember all the little details? Or would it be a conglomeration of sights, sounds, and emotions? She missed her mother when these thoughts and feelings arose, but when she saw Roxy staring with adoration into Dad's eyes, a little hiccup in the region of her heart got her attention. It was almost as if Mom was there, and the idea of Dad marrying her best friend was all part of her plan. With a little help from God, of course.

At one time she thought she would already be married and a mother by now, but it didn't happen. A little hurt in the center of her chest began to grow, but she tamped it down. She wouldn't think about her time in Texas, now. Michael had made the decision to let her go and not follow. That part of her life was over, and she'd resigned herself to the possibility of never marrying. The thought of going through such pain again wasn't worth it.

Del sniffed beside her, and she swung her head around to see her brother fighting tears. A laugh threatened to bubble up as she felt tears coming, and she slipped her hand in his. Her big brother squeezed it and smiled as he rolled his eyes at her. They weren't losing Dad. They were expanding their family in a way they never anticipated.

Whoever said redheads shouldn't wear pink?

Nick stood back, the wedding reception on the lawn of Hurricane Church in full swing, people-watching.

People-watching, my foot. Lisa-watching.

She flitted from group to group, visiting with friends and relatives, her pink dress fluttering in the summer breeze. She was beautiful.

He averted his gaze, a stab of guilt piercing his soul. Kristy would have loved this. The beautiful day, the setting of the little white church with the tabernacle and campground, an old cemetery on the hill beyond. It would have fascinated her.

Was he wrong to be here, enjoying what she would have enjoyed, without her? And looking at a beautiful woman, to boot? Kristy could have been friends with Lisa. But their paths didn't cross in the minuscule time frame of her marriage to Nick, and Lisa had been relegated to one of those distant youthful memories of college days and his best friend's little sister.

Now he saw her in a different way, and he didn't want to. It wasn't right. Besides, Del would kill him if he thought he was even noticing her in such a way. And what way was that?

As a woman. A woman who was bright, talented, beautiful, and...

"Hey, Nick, did you get enough to eat?" Lisa stood before him, smiling. It took him a few seconds to get his head back in the game it was supposed to be on.

"Plenty. Nice wedding." He cleared his throat and crossed his arms across his chest.

She put her hand on his elbow, which did nothing to lessen the ideas coming into his head. Ideas he was trying to quash. When she snatched her hand back, her face flaming, he smiled and tilted his head curiously.

Lisa chuckled and linked her fingers together. "Thanks. It's been a whirlwind, for sure. Did you know Mom and Roxy were best friends since their days at summer camp here?"

"I didn't, but funny how things turn out, isn't it?"

She shook her head. "Not funny at all. I think God had a hand in it."

"How's that?"

"Do you believe in coincidences?" Her expression was serious as she looked up at him.

Her green-eyed gaze seemed to reach all the way into his soul. "No. Maybe."

"If you believe in God, you know those are God-winks."

Nick chuckled. Cute phrase. "Now that's a new concept. Where is 'God-winks' found in the Bible?" He wished her hand was still on his arm.

Tilting her chin, she arched an eyebrow. "What about the story of Ruth?"

"What about it?" He grinned at the absolute triumph on her face.

"Do you think it was 'coincidence' that Ruth ended up in Boaz's field to glean grain?"

He narrowed his eyes at her. "Maybe, but didn't Naomi send her there?"

"Yes, but maybe it was the closest field?"

He laughed and nodded as Del walked up on crutches. "Hey Del, your sister is preaching 'God-winks' to me."

Lisa huffed. "Men. Can't live with 'em—"

Del grinned as he interrupted. "Can't live without "em, right, my friend?" Del held up his fist and Nick gave him a subtle bump.

"Whatever. You two deserve one another." Now Lisa was the one with her arms crossed in a defensive stance, but she was shaking her head and trying to hide a grin.

Nick was beginning to read her well. And he enjoyed it.

12

———⧢———

Lisa deposited Del at home following his physical therapy session, then drove up to the office. Dad's house looked so empty.

The bride and groom had flown off to Anchorage, Alaska and, on the way home, were scheduled to make their way to Seattle via cruise line, take a train from Seattle to St. Louis, then rent a car and head home. It seemed awfully complicated to her but romantic.

It made her tired thinking about so much travel.

A piece of her resented Dad for taking Roxy on the trip her mother had always dreamed about, but Dad hadn't taken a vacation since the last trip he took with Mom, almost ten years ago for their thirtieth anniversary. It was their Natchez Trace trip, driving four hundred-plus miles from Nashville, Tennessee, to Natchez, Mississippi, stopping along the way for antebellum mansion tours and random Civil War and Indian Mound sites.

Mom had been ecstatic at the thought of two whole weeks away, and oddly enough, Dad limited his work schedule for the duration. It was while Lisa and Del were both in college, so while Dad was gone, Reno Contracting shut down. Not long after they got home, Mom was diagnosed with cancer, and the roller-coaster ride of surgery, chemo, and radiation began. The Alaska trip would have been their fortieth-anniversary trip. That was Mom's plan. By their thirty-fifth, they all knew she wouldn't make it.

Lisa shook her head against the memories. It was time to make new ones. Life happened. Death came but so did new life. Her mom had grieved when she knew she wouldn't be there for Lisa and Del when they met and married the loves of their lives, and would never know her grandchildren, but they were able to spend time with her they might not have, had they been otherwise occupied.

She didn't tell her mother about Michael, and about how close she had come to bringing him home to introduce him as their new future son-in-law. It had been a whirlwind romance, the cameraman and the intern, and her employers encouraged it, hoping it would entice both of them to stay with the show. But when Mom got sick and she wanted to go home, Michael wouldn't budge. He said going home for a visit was one thing, but what could she do for her mom that the doctors and the rest of the family couldn't do?

He didn't have a clue. When she left, he told her it was over. If she came back, maybe they could talk, then.

But she didn't go back, and months later Mom died, and then another opportunity came her way that floored her.

Opening the door of the office, she set her leather portfolio bag down on the desk then sat down, chin in hand, and cried. She wanted to get it all out of her system before Dad got home. She had pushed all of it back so long it had become a part of her. *Oh, Mom, I miss you so much.* She missed belonging to someone. She missed the idea of being in love. The last few weeks had been rough.

Roxy hadn't tried to take her mother's place, and for that she was thankful. She had come along before either she or her brother had even considered Dad might be lonely for companionship. But God knew. And after his heart attack, Lisa knew he had been made aware that God had a future for him and he needed a help-meet to accomplish what needed to be done—not for Reno Construction, but for God's Kingdom.

She sat up and took a long shuddering breath as she reached for the box of tissues she had pushed behind her coloring pencils and brushes. She flipped her little devotional calendar and smiled. *Thank You, God.*

It was her favorite verse. The one she "claimed" years ago when she thought she would never find happiness and love. Teenagers had such limited vision.

Delight yourself therefore in the LORD, and He will give you the desires of your heart. Psalm 37:4

It was definitely one to hang your hat on.

She covered her face as a fresh round of tears came, this time not about her mother, but about her own loneliness. *Oh, Father, I know You have a plan for me. I know You love me and want the best for me. I've waited, depended on You for my happiness and satisfaction. Forgive me when I forget You and forge ahead without You. I've always heard it's never a good idea to pray for patience, so Lord, I'll pray for peace. How's that? I want Your peace.*

Mopping up again, she pulled her binder from her bag and opened it to Nick's project house. The measurements had been added to the spreadsheet, and now she could take her time with her drawings before consulting with the engineer.

She had been experimenting with different openings and configurations longer than she thought when she was distracted by the sound of a truck out front. With Dad gone and Del worn out from his PT session, she thought she would have the rest of the day to herself.

By the time she glanced at her face in the mirror to check for damages, then got to the door and opened it, she was surprised to see Nick waving at her as he approached.

"I didn't expect to see you here this morning."

Nick cocked a brow at her. "I tried to call, but it kept going to voicemail."

She pulled her phone from her pocket and sighed. Dead as a doornail. "I knew I was tired last night, but I never forget to charge this thing."

"Del said you were up early taking him to physical therapy."

"Yeah, and I could have charged it all the way to Paducah and back." She was irritated. She shook her head. "I'm sorry. Come on in. What did you need?"

"I got bad news today."

"Bad news? About the house?" She found her charger and plugged in her phone, all the time praying silently, *Please, don't cancel this project*. Such news would send Del over the edge.

"Indirectly." Nick grimaced. "Clay called."

Lisa put her hand on her hip and glared at him. "Surely we're not still suspects."

He chuckled briefly and shook his head. "Not likely." He took a deep breath, shoved his hands in his pockets, and settled his gaze on her. "They found another body."

Nick watched as Lisa's face flitted from thought to thought, as horror grew on her face. What must she think of him, if his grandparents' house was full of corpses? She shook her head and frowned.

"Are you...?"

"Not kidding." He shook his head.

"What in the world..."

He held up a hand. "It was further down in an offshoot from the main tunnel, and looking at the remains, has been down there for over fifty years.

"You're kidding me." She sat down on her stool, gesturing for him to take a seat next to her desk. "Well, at least we're not in the running for murdering this one." Her face scrunched in an adorable grin.

"No, I guess that's a plus."

"So, did Clay give you any information about the crime scene? Or was it an accident?"

"Pretty sure it was a crime." He couldn't keep the smirk from coming. "They found a gun and the skull had a hole in it, about the size of a bullet."

"Ouch." She rubbed her head in empathy, then dropped her chin in her hand. "Where does this put the project?"

He sighed. "Oh hold, I'm afraid." He noted the frustration on her face. This was a blow for her and Del, as well as for him.

She straightened and nodded her head. "I understand. I've kind of planned for worst-case scenario and have a few design projects I've held onto. You know, just in case."

"Yeah, me, too. I may be able to get to a new build earlier than expected, which will please the homeowners. It would get them in before cold weather."

And it would also push back his house and this opportunity to work with Lisa. By the time the old house would be available, Del would be back on his feet, and Steve would be home from his honeymoon. He would have to pay Del back another way. A stray thought came to him, but he dismissed it. No. He didn't deserve it. Concentrate on the job.

After all, if he couldn't protect Kristy, he couldn't be trusted to take care of anyone.

13

AUGUST

It had been three weeks since Lisa and Nick found a corpse in his house, two weeks since their exploration when they found interesting artifacts and a week and a half since the wedding of the year–the wedding of Steve and Roxy Reno. A little over a week since Nick had put the project on hold because of a second corpse found in the tunnels beneath his property. Lisa pondered all that was happening, and she was ready for things to return to normal, whatever "normal" was.

Dad and Roxy would be gone for another three weeks, Del was in a brace for another month, and she was trying to work on two decorating jobs at a time.

With everything going on, she hadn't talked to Nick in over a week. Funny, it was that fact setting her train of thought in motion.

Enough. She had enough to do taking care of Del, keeping the business going, and getting used to the idea of having an extended family of Roxy, Roxy's daughter Darcy, and those sweet toddlers, Benji and Ally. They always brought a smile to her face. Since the night of Dad's heart attack and Benji's bump on the noggin, Ally had claimed her, and Benji not long after. She was now "Aunt Lisa," and she loved it.

Chin in hand, she scrolled through the website full of baby

furniture and decor. She sighed. It was a great gig, decorating the nursery for her best friend, Melanie York. She'd always dreamed of decorating her own nursery. Why she envisioned it at the top of the stairs of a certain craftsman farmhouse not far from the Ohio River, she couldn't imagine.

She slapped the laptop closed and pulled out the Bible lying on her desk under a stack of manila file folders. She'd neglected her quiet time. There was so much to *do*, it seemed.

In Matthew, where she was reading, Jesus tells the story of "The Good Samaritan," which was heart-warming, but then, in the next chapter, He talks about the Pharisees and how they were "white-washed sepulchers." White-washed tombs. Pretty on the outside, but selfish and unpleasant on the inside.

Was she a white-washed tomb? Had she begun concentrating more on her outward appearance, her position in the community, and the way people *saw* her, rather than allowing people to see Jesus through her?

She thought about the old Woodward homestead site. The old house, when it was there, had stood on a hill, overlooking the river. Anyone coming down the river, or coming up the hill, could see the house. At one time it was a beacon. A place where people could find sanctuary. When river traffic became less important, it may have become a place where criminals hid their wares. She guessed even a house could be a "white-washed sepulcher."

In chapter ten, the middle of what she was reading, she found Mary and Martha. Martha, bustling about trying to get dinner on the table for their guest of honor, Jesus, and Mary, sitting at his feet and drinking in his teaching. Martha fussed, and Jesus took Mary's side.

Lisa grinned. Was she turning into Martha? So much to do, so little time to do it? Was she so intent on proving herself, making sure everyone knew she could accomplish more than they expected that she neglected the good things in life? Enjoying her family? Opening her heart to love?

She closed her Bible and shut her eyes. Her prayers of late had been snatches of "help me" and "thank You, God," but now she wanted to rest in Him. To unleash those "groanings which cannot be uttered" that only God can hear.

The phone on her desk began to vibrate, pulling her from her meditation on God's word. She picked it up as she bit her lip.

It was Nick.

Nick hesitated to call. It had been a week since he'd seen her, talked to her, but he hadn't gone a day without thinking about her—well, about the project. He'd go with that.

This new discovery in the house was too exciting not to share. He'd love to spend a few days doing nothing but exploring the mysteries of the tunnel, but the homeowner of the lake house he'd recently contracted to build might not be on board.

He pulled out his cell phone and hit "recents" icon where he found her number from when they'd talked last week. Maybe he should text first? No. Too much for a text.

He tapped her name and pulled the phone to his ear as he stood on the back porch, staring in the direction of the river. You could see the hazy horizon, which was the other side of the Ohio River, in Illinois. The breeze smelled of a combination of muddy water and pollen, and he loved it. Always had.

After a couple of rings, she picked up.

"Hi, Nick."

Was it his imagination, or could he *hear* her smile? "Hey, Lisa, how are you?"

"Great! You?"

"I'm out at the house."

"Your house?"

"Yeah. Clay called me when they found another leg of the tunnel."

"Have they released the house yet?"

"Nope, but they've found some interesting things." He didn't want to give it away too soon.

"And?"

"And, I thought maybe you might want to meet me out here one day and do a little exploring."

Nothing. Had she lost interest? She was probably busy and he'd interrupted her.

"Nick? Are you there?"

"Yeah."

"Oh good. My phone blanked out for a second." She laughed. "Or yours did. I seem to remember reception isn't optimal out there."

He felt his lips stretch into a slow smile. "Yeah, if I decide to live out here, I'll need to do a little research."

"I would love to go exploring—provided there aren't any more bodies?"

"No more bodies. They won't let us work on the house, or in the basement where the tunnel starts, but they did find the other end of a new tunnel where the skeletal remains were found."

"Seriously?" She sounded intrigued.

"Seriously. Clay said as long as we don't disturb what is blocked off with crime-scene tape, we may explore all we want to."

"Is it safe?"

"I think so. I went through part of it, and it seemed pretty firm."

Was she chewing on her bottom lip? It was one of her little quirks that intrigued him.

She definitely had paused this time.

"Look, if you can't..."

"No, I want to. I'm checking my calendar. I've got a shopping trip planned with a client tomorrow, but maybe Saturday?"

"I guess you know this whole 'married, with children' thing is putting a dent in our friendship."

Traveling north on Highway Sixty to Evansville, Indiana, Lisa chuckled as she glanced at her very pregnant friend.

"Hey, let's be thankful I was able to get away for the day." Melanie sighed with pleasure and wriggled herself into the leather seat of the nicer-than-average Ford King Ranch pickup truck.

"Oh, believe me, I am!"

With her dad out of town, Lisa took his truck so she could haul today's purchased items for Melanie's nursery. It had to be ready in three months, preferably sooner. Melanie and Jake had a two-year-old, and no one was surprised when they announced the imminent arrival of child number two.

Mel turned her dark brown eyes to Lisa. "I'm also very thankful you were able to get to me earlier than you thought. When your first baby is three weeks early, you learn to plan better for the second one."

"One thing's for sure, if I didn't have the nursery ready, he or she would come when ready, anyway." Lisa grinned and raised an eyebrow in suspicion. "What did you say it was, this time? Boy or girl?"

"No clue." Mel laughed. "With Emily, we knew pretty early on, but this time, when we can actually afford to create a nursery that isn't filled with hand-me-downs? No reason to do the extra ultrasound telling us if we've got a 'he' or a 'she'!"

"I can handle decorating blind as long as it's not just me in the dark."

"No, if I knew, you would definitely know. Have I ever been able to keep anything a secret?" Mel shook her head. "I'm way too easy."

"It's always been one of your more endearing qualities, in my book."

"Yeah, well." Mel rolled her eyes. "Makes it more exciting, in a way. Jake would love to find out, but it's kinda fun to think both ways, you know?"

Lisa's laugh bubbled out. "No, I don't, but maybe someday, I will."

"You will, Lisa. No question about it." Mel closed her eyes and smiled. "I love my baby girl so much, you know I do."

Lisa quirked an eyebrow and glanced over. "Yes, and?"

"I'm enjoying my day without her. Does that mean I'm a terrible mother, or is it the hormones talking?"

"Hormones, definitely."

"Good." Mel sat up suddenly. "Oh! Did I tell you Emily used the potty the other day?"

"You did." Lisa laughed out loud. "In fact, you sent me a text and a picture."

"Oh yeah. I'm so proud of her. She actually asked to go."

"Bordering on TMI, Mel."

"Someday you'll be calling me every time your kid burps."

"Probably." Lisa lapsed into silence. It scared her a little, the idea of having a family without her mom. She kept telling herself people did it all the time, and she could, too. Not much point worrying about it. One needed a husband to have a family, or at least in her world they did.

"Are you busy this weekend?"

There it was. The fix-up. She knew it was coming.

"It depends. If it's anything but a blind date, I'm available. Otherwise, I'm washing my hair. I do have plans on Saturday."

"Haha." Mel turned a frustrated look on her friend. "It's not so much a blind date as dinner with friends and a potential new friend. Jake's cousin, not from here. We wouldn't even have to leave town, if you're worried about how late we might be."

"Oh, it's not the leaving town I have a problem with. It's the awkward silences."

"Come now. You? Awkward?" Mel stifled a giggle.

"Cute. You know I'm the queen of awkward."

Mel sighed. "True. You never did grow out of the accident-prone stage. But you look good."

"Well, we all know that's what's important." She laughed as she pulled in to the parking lot in front of Bedland Kids to shop for a convertible youth bed for Emily and a crib for baby number two.

"It doesn't hurt. You've got all this amazing red hair—hair people will pay big bucks to acquire—and you're cute as can be either 'au naturel' or when you fix up like today."

"It's obvious you never got called 'carrot-top' as a child or was never mistaken as fifteen at twenty-five." Lisa unbuckled her seatbelt and grabbed her notes.

Mel struggled to find the seatbelt fastener, and Lisa pulled it up so she could see it around her girth. "Thanks. Of course not. Dark brown is as common as dirt, and by the time I was twenty-five I was married and pregnant. I think it was the mom-van that gave me away." She turned and slid out of the truck onto her feet with a grunt and met Lisa around the front of the vehicle.

Lisa put her hands on her hips and gave her friend a glare that brooked no argument. "Yeah. Well. I defy anyone who would compare your luxurious mahogany-colored hair with dirt."

"Well if you love me so much, come over for supper tomorrow night. Deal?" Mel gave Lisa a cheesy grin.

Hands in the air, Lisa gave up. "Fine. What time, and what can I bring?" She turned before opening the door to Bedland. "I forgot to ask you who it was."

Mel frowned. "I don't know how you'd know him. I only see him at family things, but he's been working around here and he and Jake reconnected." She shrugged. "It's Jake's cousin that lives in Kuttawa. Nick Woodward."

This time the laugh didn't bubble out. It exploded.

<hr />

"You're my 'mystery date'?" Nick took one look at the beautiful redhead at the door and laughed out loud.

"Seriously?" Lisa sputtered with laughter. "Jake didn't tell you who it was?"

Jake walked into the room carrying the beautiful blonde toddler who was reaching out to Lisa. "Aw, I knew you knew each other. I was just messin' with Mel and Nick."

"And they say women are conniving." Melanie came to the kitchen door, spatula in hand, shaking her head. "Fortunately for Jake, I found out yesterday."

Nick shook his head and grinned. This might turn out to be a good fix-up after all.

"We're related on my mom's side, so Nick spent more time in this part of the state than I did, as a kid, at his dad's parents' place."Jake relinquished little Emily to Lisa and turned to Mel. "We live in a small community, my dear. What are the odds two people in the construction business wouldn't have run across one another?" He gave his wife a kiss on the cheek, then straightened and rubbed his hands together. "What can I do to help you get this show on the road? Some of us have worked hard today." He winked at his guests.

"You seriously said that to the woman who is carrying your child?" Mel, hands on hips, turned to Lisa. "I've changed my mind. I want the expensive baby bed instead."

"No way." Lisa shook her head and considered her friend matter-of-factly. "You'd have buyer's remorse within an hour."

"How much was this expensive baby bed? And how much is the one you picked out?" Jake raised an eyebrow and tilted his head toward his lovely wife.

She batted her eyes and gave him a big smile. "Oh, you mean the one that's literally branded 'Million Dollar Baby?' It's only twelve hundred dollars."

He blanched. "Tell me that's the expensive one?"

Lisa laughed. "Of course it is." She patted Jake on the arm. "I'll take care of your budget."

"So how much is the one we're actually getting?" His voice held concern.

"One eighty-nine." Mel put her hands on her hips and raised herself to her full height. "Satisfied?"

He let out a deep breath and mopped his brow of faux sweat. "Whew. I didn't think Lisa would steer you wrong, but you never know, when two women get together on a shopping trip."

Lisa raised her eyebrows at Mel. "This means war, doesn't it?"

Mel arched a brow. "Oh, definitely. Trivial Pursuit will be girls against boys this time."

"Sorry Nick, you're stuck with Jake." Lisa shook her head slowly.

"Is that a bad thing?"

"Depends on whether or not you want to win." Mel gave him a saccharine smile.

"Maybe Nick will pull us both to the winner's circle. You never know." Jake was a little sheepish. "I'm terrible at this game."

Nick smiled and rubbed his hands together. "Classic or updated?"

"Classic, of course. Mel found it at a thrift store."

"Then it's a good thing I'm here. Boys against girls? We can take them, cousin."

"In the meantime, lasagna is ready, and the salad is ready to be put on the table. Lisa?" Mel led her into the dining room of the sprawling ranch-style house. "Food first, competition later."

14

Lisa opened the door of her cottage and looked back. Nick had followed her home from Mel and Jake's house and waited until he saw her door open before he pulled away. She smiled and waved, then made her way into the house, watching to make sure she didn't trip over a cat in the process.

Purse and keys deposited on the little table beside the door, she glanced around her little house and sighed.

It was a cute place. Minuscule, but cute. Perfect for one without going to the extreme of "tiny house" living. The small living room held a small sofa, a chair and ottoman, and a rocking chair, no room for a coffee table, so instead, she had two tiny occasional tables in the center of the room. They could move out if she needed the space.

Fortunately, Lisa preferred minimalism when it came to decorative items, because with three cats in an eight hundred-square-foot house, everything would have ended up on the floor, anyway.

Elspeth and Dougal, her tabby and tuxedo cats respectively, looked up from where they were curled on the sofa. Jack was somewhere. Most likely sleeping under the bed.

"Hey, babies, did you miss me?" She sat on the vacant section of the couch and patted her lap. No response. She laughed. "Am I bothering you?"

She checked the clock and gave them each a pat. "It's time to go to bed. I have a date in the morning."

Was it a date? Of course, it wasn't. Nick was smart to have someone along when exploring the tunnels. It was a safety measure. Had to be. She was just Del's little sister, and even though they were part of a fix-up tonight, it didn't mean anything. Two friends hanging out because they had no one else, and nothing else going on.

She was available.

And, she was highly interested to see what could be in a tunnel underneath a hundred-year-old house.

This area along the Ohio River was known for its nefarious history, including river pirates, the Trail of Tears, and many incidences that had never been recorded. In the 1800s, it had been the Wild West and didn't get much tamer until the railroad, and then electricity came along with the Rural Electrification Act.

Her mind switched from Nick to the historical significance of his house. Then back to Nick. He hadn't changed much since college. Quieter, maybe, but then he'd been through a lot. To lose a spouse at such a young age had to do a number on you. She shook her head. She'd always had the dream of finding Mr. Right and settling down to raise a family, and living to old age. Most people had such a dream. Nick's had been cut short when he lost a wife and child in one random traffic accident.

Would she be interested in someone who had experienced all that before her? She wasn't sure. There was a tiny bit of her that was jealous. Not of his tragedy, but of the experiences he'd had and she had not. Her dream didn't account for such.

Her dream had always had her and her dream man experiencing all the highs and lows the first time, together.

Nick tossed and turned in the wide, empty bed. He drifted off to sleep only to dream of driving through the countryside in the darkness, waving as he left a house and, as he left, the house exploding.

"That's it." He got up and paced a few minutes, forcing himself awake so he wouldn't go right back into the same dream. It seemed like a combination of Kristy's accident and his evening with Lisa. Was Lisa the person he waved at in the dream? Was she in the explosion?

He padded into the kitchen and picked up the coffee pot. Minnie lifted her head from her bed between the living room and kitchen, then snuffled and went back to sleep. The carafe still had about a cup in it from the morning before. He poured it and placed the mug in the microwave and pushed the button for "quick minute."

He sat at the kitchen table and reached for his Bible, which still sat there from church last Sunday. He had neglected the Word and had shunned all but the outward appearance of being a Christian. He opened it to First John. He was getting close to the end of the New Testament, and had in the past loved the letters written by Paul, Peter, and John the best. He used to imagine they were written to him. Now he read it with a skeptical eye and a sore heart.

He read the introduction, then a few chapters. He got to chapter four and had to stop and think when he got to verses eighteen and nineteen.

There is no fear in love, but perfect love casts out fear because fear involves torment. But he who fears has not been made perfect in love. We love Him because He first loved us.

Was he fearful? If not, why was the dream so real he had to get up? John was right. Fear is torment. It starts nibbling away at you when something happens, and eventually makes a dent in the armor you build around yourself.

Before Kristy's accident, he was on top of the world. He had a beautiful wife, expecting his first child, and his business was taking off like gangbusters. He had big plans. God had been good to him.

His mind flitted to the Parable of the Rich Fool. He put his hand in

First John and flipped back to Luke, searching until he found it.

There. Luke, chapter twelve. Jesus told the story to his disciples and the crowd that gathered anywhere he went. A rich man had a bumper crop and knew he wouldn't have room to store his grain, so he made plans to tear down his barns and build bigger ones, little knowing he would die that very night. Who would benefit from all his wealth? Reading further in the chapter, Nick noted that Jesus followed up by telling his disciples not to fear. God provided for their needs, and they needed only to listen to Him.

Nick closed his Bible and rubbed his face with weary hands as he stood and made his way to his recliner. Kristy had called it his "dad chair," and shook her head when he begged for it, but gave in, as usual. He should have done more giving in for her.

He was stuck. Pure and simple. He hadn't made progress forward or backward since Kristy died. He was in a holding pattern: get up, go to work, come home, go to bed, and start it all over again. As if altering that pattern would let loose some kind of curse he knew better than to believe in.

He'd read the articles. Losing a spouse was a traumatic event. It was stressful, and it induced guilt, which was the last thing Kristy would want for him.

Was God telling him to move on? To get out of the hamster wheel he was in?

Last night was fun. It was the first time in a long time he hadn't backed off of a social situation. If he hadn't been cajoled into reconnecting with his cousin, he would never have agreed to it. He'd let go and enjoyed himself and the company he was in. What was intended to be a fix-up by Mel ended up being simply a good time with good friends.

A friend he had a date with tomorrow.

It wasn't a date. Why was Lisa the first person he thought of when

Clay told him he could explore the tunnels? Maybe because Del had a broken leg? He could have asked Jake or anyone.

But he'd asked Lisa. Sitting in the darkness, stretched out in his recliner, he felt a wave of sleepiness come over him, and he took a deep, cleansing breath. Smiling, he realized he was excited about spending time with someone who had the potential to get him out of his own head.

15

Nick handed Lisa a cappuccino when she finished buckling her seat belt.

"Thanks so much." She took a tentative sip and closed her eyes in pleasure. "What is it about convenience-store coffee?"

"It can go either way." He backed out of her driveway carefully, checking both ways before entering the street in downtown Clementville. "I've had my best, and my worst, cups of coffee at convenience stores."

"Must not have been the Five Star in Marion, then. I've never gotten a bad cup of coffee there."

"Nope. I won't mention the name, but the worst I ever had tasted like it had been burning in the bottom of the machine all night and hadn't had a new filter in a few years."

"That's unfortunate." She wrinkled her nose. "This, on the other hand, is heavenly."

"I thought you might enjoy it."

"Very astute of you." She took another sip. "So, what did they find down there? What's the big mystery? I've been coming up with all kinds of scenarios."

He glanced at her with a smile as he drove. "Like what?" The artist in her had probably come up with some doozies.

She placed her cup in the cup holder and touched her finger to her chin. "Underground railroad was one idea. Then bootleggers.

Ghosts?" She cut her eyes at him. "Am I close?"

"You're close. Very close." He chuckled. "Well, except for the ghost part." The warmth of her presence was seeping into him. His dark night of the soul might have led, literally, to joy in the morning.

He pulled into the driveway and around to the back of the house, and down the lane to the home-place where they had entered the tunnel before. "I need to get gravel hauled. This dry spell won't last forever."

"Sometimes it seems like it." She grinned. "Until the unrelenting rain sets in."

"Yeah." He got out of the truck and pocketed his phone, then noted Lisa's sensible attire. "Good call on the hiking boots."

"And old jeans." She brushed imaginary dust off well-worn Levis as she met him around the front of the truck. "The ones I had on when I fell through the porch haven't been the same since."

"I'll try to avoid having you go across rotting timber."

"I appreciate the thought." From where they walked she could see a tiny bit of the roofline. "Are we going in through the old cellar?"

Hauling a backpack out of the rear of the cab, he crooked his finger to have her follow him and took off past the decrepit fireplace ruin and down a path toward the Ohio River. "I want to go in from the other end that the detectives found."

"I feel a little bit like Tom Sawyer and Huckleberry Finn."

He held a bramble back for her to go into the less-traveled pathway. "I didn't bring my tools to build a raft, so we'll have to depend on our own two feet for this trip."

They walked past the clearing where they had entered before, up the bluff, and then descended down the bank. Nick kept a close watch on Lisa. The last thing he wanted to happen was for her to get hurt. "When I saw the opening from the top, it didn't seem to be as steep as this."

"Oh, it looked as steep." She puffed a bit when she ended up on a flat spot.

"Afraid of heights?"

"If it were straight down I would be, but this isn't too bad." She stood next to Nick, searching the area. "Where is the opening?"

He smiled at her as she looked around, confused. "Whoever did this concealed it well."

"Too well. I don't know how the detectives ever found it."

"It helps if you find it from the other end." He had to laugh.

"Well of course." She gestured for him to proceed. "I'll follow you, provided you know where it is."

He pulled back a large tree branch and there it was, a hole big enough for a crouching human to walk through. "I can't promise you we won't find wildlife in there."

"As long as there are no more corpses, I'll be fine."

"I've got my pellet gun on me, just in case." He patted his pocket. "Somebody mentioned bats, but nothing else."

"What about black bears? I've heard of them swimming across the river near here."

"Nah, the forensics team didn't mention anything about signs, so we should be good."

"I'm glad. They're cute." She raised her eyebrows at him pointedly. "From a distance."

"I agree." He raised his brows. She seemed a little nervous. "Are you ready?"

"As ready as I'll ever be."

The flashlight beam flickered on the brick and dirt walls that occasionally glittered with the odd piece of spar, lead, and calcite riddling the earth in this part of the country. Lisa walked carefully, glad Nick was walking ahead of her, catching any cobwebs or stray roots sticking out. It made her think of the beginning of a scary movie, and there was no way she would have come down here alone. Her imagination was too good.

"You okay back there?" Nick swung around and shined the flashlight on her, avoiding her eyes.

"I was thinking that in a horror flick the girl would be alone, and I would be screaming for her to turn back." She wrinkled her nose in embarrassment as an involuntary shiver raised the hair on her arms. *Why am I such a fraidy-cat?*

He laughed out loud, his voice echoing through the chamber. They must be close to a wider opening. "And here I thought I brought you along to protect me."

"Very funny. I haven't seen any offshoots yet. You mentioned they found bats?"

"It's further up, between where we found the corpse and here." Nick turned and resumed walking further into the tunnel.

"Whatever happened to the mama cat and kittens?" Ooops. Her foot slipped on loose rocks. Watch it, silly girl.

He heard her stumble and turned, raising his eyebrows at her sheepish look.

"I'm fine. I didn't even go down this time."

"This time?"

"You've heard the idiom, 'a day without whatever is like a day without sunshine'?"

"Yes." He chuckled softly.

"Well for me, a day without falling down is a red-letter day."

"Is it really that bad?"

"No, but ask anybody. I'm notorious for getting lost in my own thoughts and plowing into stuff." She twisted her lips and raised a finger to make her point. "Except for when I'm driving. I'm actually a very good driver."

"Good. I hated to think you were completely down on yourself and your abilities."

They continued further underground into the tunnel, the angle of descent finally leveling off.

"I think we're pretty close."

"But to what?"

"You'll see." He turned and grinned back at her. "Look on the walls."

There was a series of oil lamps affixed to the walls, near the ceiling of the tunnel.

"That's new."

"Or really old." He waggled his brows.

"You know what I mean." She shook her head.

As they spoke, they arrived at a larger room, hollowed out of the earth and lined with bricks. Nick didn't say anything, but simply shined his light around the room.

"Whoa."

"You took the words right out of my mouth. Nick put his backpack on the ground and pulled out a lantern. "Maybe this will help from here on."

"Good. I'll carry the flashlight if you want."

"Can't have too much light."

Lisa slowly guided the beam of light around the perimeter of the room, stopped at a door, and then at something in the far corner. "What's that?"

"Let's find out." He took the lantern, held it high, and led her to the object. Squatting in front of it, he examined the conglomeration of metal pieces.

"Is it...?" Surely not. But maybe?

He touched the tubing leading from a vat. "I do believe it is." He looked up at her. "I've inherited an authentic moonshine still. I guess this explains some of the other stuff we found."

"I've seen the still Hawkeye and Trapper John made on *M*A*S*H*, and I've seen replicas, but I've never seen one in person"

Nick scratched his head. He knew pre-Prohibition bootlegging was common in the area, and still was in remote areas, but here was proof the illegal activity was close to home.

"Interesting." He rubbed on the metal still, revealing the copper underneath the patina. "Looks like maybe a thirty-gallon container stacked up on the bricks." He stood, raking his hand through his dark hair.

Lisa walked around, shining her light in the corners of the room. "Nothing else in here."

Nick nodded. "I imagine whoever had this was able to get their moonshine out before they got caught. I'm surprised the still remains in here, though."

"Yeah, usually the revenuers took everything and destroyed it. I've seen old pictures of the revenue agents with piles of the stuff." Lisa picked up the curled tube of copper that made up part of the apparatus.

"Let's go in a little further." He picked up the lantern and raised it, moving toward the closed door.

Lisa followed. "Do you have any idea how far we are from the first room we found?"

He pulled out his phone. "We can't be too far. I set my distance app on my phone when we entered the tunnel, and we've already gone nearly a half mile."

He opened the door, holding the lantern in front of him as Lisa came up behind him. "There's a sort of hallway tunnel, then another door."

It was narrower, and there were no lanterns on the wall as there had been earlier. It smelled musty as if there hadn't been any fresh air in this corridor in a long time.

"Is it me, or is it a little claustrophobic in here?" Lisa's voice was a whisper.

He could tell she was sticking close behind him. "It's not just you. Does it seem like we've turned somewhere?"

"I thought so, but I've lost all concept of direction down here."

Nick pulled up his distance app. "We must be closer to the surface here. I've got a signal."

"Really?" She checked hers. "I do, too, but barely."

"It shows we're now heading west."

"So we have changed direction."

"The door out of the last room was on the left."

"We were paying so much attention to the still we didn't notice we veered off."

"Probably." Nick paused at the door. "After we get as far as we can, I want to see if there's another opening out of the room that would have been a straighter shot from the original cellar."

"Sounds exciting. But first, let's see what's behind door number two, shall we?" Lisa's eyes sparkled in the lantern light.

He nodded and smiled at her. It was nice to be on an adventure with a partner. He'd been a loner too long. "We shall."

He rotated the knob, and the door stuck a little. Reasonable, considering the moisture he could feel in the air. After a little pushing, he shoved it with his shoulder and it gave way. He heard scurrying in the darkness. Maybe Lisa hadn't heard it. She suddenly clutched his arm.

Nope. She'd heard it.

"What was that?"

He held the lantern up to illuminate more area and found yet another room, this one smaller than either of the other rooms. "I think I've found our culprit." He took the flashlight from Lisa and shone it into a corner where an old trunk was lying on its side. Glowing eyes shone in the shadows.

"It's Mama Cat!" Lisa took the lantern from his hands and crept toward the frightened feline. She stopped and knelt, lowering her voice. "It's okay, Mama Cat, you can come out." She put her hand out and patiently waited as the tabby came toward her. "Remember me?"

"She's not wild, that's for sure." Nick chuckled gently as the cat allowed Lisa to pick her up, stroking her hair and scratching behind her ears.

"Definitely not." She smiled up at Nick. "And if Mama Cat is here, babies can't be far behind."

"Detective Reed left the carrier up in the house. I didn't even think to pick it up." He hung the lantern on a hook on the ceiling to spread the light around further.

Lisa hesitated. "If we find them, we could carry them up, I suppose, although the kittens might be pretty wild, even if Mama Cat isn't."

"If I recall, kittens have very sharp little claws."

"They do." At a soft mewing in the distance, Mama Cat leaped from her arms. "Is this where they found the counterfeit ten?"

Nick nodded in the affirmative. "They had Treasury Department guys down here last week."

"The FBI was here? How cool is that?" Lisa's eyes opened wider.

"Pretty cool." He laughed.

"I'm surprised they let us come this far."

"The evidence in this part of the tunnel was so old it didn't take them long to clear it. Plus, the FBI is a little quicker than state and local law enforcement."

"I can only imagine." Lisa huffed. "Clay used to want to be in the FBI, but was afraid of the physical fitness requirement." She arched a brow at Nick. "The Internet can be a scary thing."

"I don't blame him. I knew a guy who was determined to get into the FBI, and he trained like crazy for over a year to be able to pass it. I saw his mom not too long ago. I asked how he was doing, and she said he wouldn't tell her anything, because then he'd have to kill her." Nick gave an absentminded laugh as he shone his flashlight around a rickety wooden desk in the corner. He started pulling out drawers, and one stuck. "Wonder how long this has been here?"

He struggled with it and got it to open partway. When he reached inside to see what was holding it up, he felt the wooden back of the drawer. "Something's not right. This drawer isn't as deep as the others."

Lisa bent over and shone the light inside the shallow drawer. "There's a hole in the wood." Her eyes were wide when she looked up. "False back?"

"Let's find out." He took out his Swiss Army knife and pulled out the multi-purpose hook. "Don't leave home without it."

"I should get one of those. It would take up less room in my purse than my five-in-one tool."

He reached in and tried the hole with his finger, but it was too small. With the hook, he was able to get it to give a little, then suddenly Nick went sprawling, the drawer coming out in his hand.

"You'd think the damp would have ruined this by now." He brushed himself off as he picked up the drawer and placed it on the top of the desk.

Lisa opened the small container attached to the drawer and pulled out a small book. "I'm surprised they didn't find this." She opened it, then looked up at Nick. "It's a journal, Nick."

"Let me see." He walked around to stand next to her under the lantern, and shone the flashlight directly on it. The paper was fragile. "We need to take this aboveground."

"Yeah, you don't want it to disintegrate down here."

He placed it carefully in a bag inside his backpack.

"Good call bringing a bag with you." Lisa nodded, then turned back to him in excitement. "Hey, we could put the cats in there."

He paused and then shook his head. "No, I'm not going to traumatize them by stuffing them in a backpack. We'll get them when we can come in from the other side."

"Probably a better plan."

16

Lisa watched as Nick gently pulled the small volume from the plastic zipper bag, then laid it on paper towels on her conference table at the Reno-Vations office.

She heard Nick's stomach rumble. It was one o'clock, past lunchtime. "Are you sure you don't want to go get something to eat before we dig into this?"

"No way. I at least want to get a sense of what time period we're talking about." He patted his stomach as it rumbled yet again. "Got any water?"

Lisa grinned and walked over to the mini-frig in the corner. "Coming right up." She held up a small packet. "Jerky?"

"Perfect."

"You snack, I'll turn the pages."

"Carefully."

"Of course." She narrowed here eyes at him and sat in the chair next to him. "I'm only clumsy when I'm on my feet."

Lisa took a paper towel and wiped some dust, dirt, and mold from the cover, then carefully opened it to the flyleaf. The yellowed page had various marks on it, numbers written as if it were used for scratch paper for quick figures. "Can you make out the name at the top?" The brown ink had all but disappeared as it aged.

Nick got closer to the book and shook his head. "Do you have a magnifying glass?"

She went to her desk and rummaged through the top drawer. "I know there was at some point. She took out the tray holding her supplies and dug into the back of the drawer, then pulled out the elusive object. "Here it is."

"Thanks." Nick held it to the faint writing. "Is that an 's'?"

"Let me see." Lisa adjusted it and peered down at what appeared to be a signature. "Salina?"

"Looks like it. Can you make out the last name?"

She went over to her desk and unplugged her task light, replugging it in the outlet next to the table. "Maybe this will help." Positioning it where it shone directly on the page, she took the magnifying glass and gazed at the name. "Crofton. Salina Crofton."

"My great-grandmother?" Nick shook his head.

Lisa pondered. "Probably, but Crofton is a common name in the area. Not so much now, but years ago, it was. I think I may be related to them, too."

"No kidding?"

"Who knows, maybe we're related?" Lisa raised an eyebrow and grinned.

An expression of horror crossed Nick's face. "I hope not."

"Hey." Would it be so terrible to be related to her?

He seemed to rethink his reaction. "It would mean I was related to Del."

"Yeah, yeah. I get it. You don't want to be responsible for me." She felt her face redden. She'd rather he didn't want to be related to her for more personal reasons.

"Anyway, we now have the name of the owner of this little book. Let's see what's inside."

Lisa carefully turned the page. "Do you see anything that looks like a date?"

"Here you go." He read it aloud.

"4 June 1924. A hundred and fifty gallons. Mr. Black. 589 N. Market. Chicago. Twenty-five dollars a gallon"

He stopped reading and stood straighter, looking at her.

Lisa stared back. "Nick."

"I know. This isn't just about counterfeit money."

She could feel the excitement bubbling up inside her. "Oh, Nick, this is fascinating."

He turned more pages. "There aren't many records, but here are a few more."

"I was thinking the Underground Railroad, but it seems as if there was more going on here." Lisa glanced at Nick, then at her desk where the floorplan of the house lay.

He nodded in agreement. "The addition where the kitchen is was built with the basement."

Her eyes flicked up to his. "So they wouldn't lose access to the tunnels."

"I wouldn't be surprised." Nick put his hands in his pockets. "I want you to keep this here."

"Are you sure? It's yours, after all."

"I know, but any research that needs to be done will be done here, and I want to keep it close to where it belongs."

"Do you think this is connected to the more recent crime?" Her excitement was turning to a sick feeling in the pit of her stomach.

"Very possibly." He glanced down at the small book. "Looks like I need to talk to Clay again, maybe ask him what the FBI agents found."

She nodded, glad she wasn't alone in this venture. Somehow, knowing she was working on this with Nick gave her a thrill of anticipation, but her stomach grumbled with hunger instead of nerves. "Now can we eat?"

His smile warmed her heart. He relaxed, looked down at the book, then back at her. "I think a discovery like this deserves the best burger in town, don't you, Nancy Drew?"

"I agree, Joe Hardy."

The friendly jingle of the bell on the door to the Clementville Café was mirrored by the smile on Darcy's face when Lisa saw her stepsister.

"Hey, Lisa!"

Lisa reached out to hug her. She'd always wanted a little sister, and now she had one. "Have you met Nick?"

"I think so? Weren't you at the wedding?" Darcy narrowed her eyes a bit, then raised a brow as she glanced from Lisa to Nick and back again.

"I was. Del and I went to college together."

"I see."

Lisa noted Darcy's heightened color at the mention of her big brother. She grinned at the thought of those two together. Did "siblings" count if they're steps, and they didn't become such until adulthood? Something to ponder for another day. Today was about celebrating their discovery.

Darcy held out her hand. "Well, since we didn't meet officially at the wedding, I'm Darcy Sloan, Roxy's daughter."

"Nice to meet you, Darcy. Nick Woodward." He shook her hand and smiled.

"Oh, Lisa! I've got something for you. Don't let me forget and I'll bring it to you at the table." She picked up two menus and two sets of silverware. "I'll put you at the table by the window."

Lisa and Nick followed her, and Lisa continued talking. "I'm intrigued, now. Hints?"

"Nope, it's a surprise." Darcy laughed. "Oh, and I talked to Mom last night."

"How are the newlyweds?"

They settled into the booth and a teenage girl brought them each a glass of ice water.

Darcy glanced at the girl and smiled. "Thanks, Lily."

"You're welcome." Lily turned to Lisa and Nick. "I'll be back in a few minutes when you've had time to check the menu."

Nick grinned. "If we even need to look. I know what I want. You?"

"What's the special today?"

"Cheeseburger and loaded fries."

Lisa closed the menu and handed it to the waitress. "You know I can't resist. Cheeseburger, dressed, and loaded fries. And I'll have a ginger ale with that, please."

Nick looked at the beverage portion of the menu. "Same for me, but make it a chocolate shake."

"You are celebrating, aren't you?" Lisa smiled broadly, then remembered that Darcy was still with them. "How are the parents?"

"They're great. They went hiking on a glacier and saw a pod of whales. I could hear your dad in the background telling her things to tell me."

"Sounds like they're having a good time." Lisa reached out and took Darcy's hand. "I'm glad they found each other."

"I know. Talk about hiding in plain sight."

"God had a plan, even when we were hurting." Lisa searched Darcy's eyes. "He has a plan for all of us, you know."

Darcy took a deep breath and smiled, a little too brightly. "That's what I hear." She squeezed Lisa's hand. "I'd better get to work. This place won't run itself, you know."

"Your mom will be proud. This place is hoppin'!"

"Let's hope it stays this way. I'll be back in a minute with your surprise."

As Darcy walked away, Lily brought out their drinks and straws.

Lisa opened her straw and placed it in her ginger ale. Stirring the ice in her drink, she wondered what it would take to get Darcy to open up to her. She knew she was hurting. Raising two children alone had to be hard. No two ways about it. Even with friends and family, it was difficult.

She glanced up to see Darcy wending her way to their booth with a package, and a raised eyebrow meant only for her, she knew.

Darcy rushed back to the table after seating customers and disappearing for what seemed like two seconds. "I wanted to bring this to you before you got away or I forgot." She presented the box with a simple ribbon tied around it.

Lisa tilted her head and accepted the gift with a thank you, then immediately untied the ribbon. She opened the box, separated the tissue paper, and felt tears come to her eyes. She looked up at Darcy. "Thank you so much. You didn't have to do this." The framed photo, taken at Dad and Roxy's wedding, pictured their blended family of Dad, Roxy, Darcy and her little ones, Benji and Addy, herself, and Del. "It's perfect, and I'll cherish it."

"I've got one for Del, too." Darcy's face flushed. "I'll get it to him sometime."

"He'll appreciate it." Lisa showed the picture to Nick.

"We need to get together when the parents get home and look at all of them. They sent the link to the website, but I didn't want to look at all of them until Mom and Steve got home. I had to see the ones with the kids, though."

"I don't blame you." Lisa laughed as she focused on at Benji and Addy. "Benji looks like he's plotting something, doesn't he?"

"Oh, I'm sure he is. That boy." Darcy shook her head.

"They're cute kids. How old are they?" Nick glanced up from the happy image.

"They're two years old. Three in November, and into everything."

Nick was quiet. Was he thinking he should have had a two-year-old at this point? Lisa spoke up. "Did I tell you I'm their favorite aunt?"

"Are you, now?" He grinned, but there was a shadow in his eyes.

"Considering you're their only aunt, I don't think the competition was very stiff."

They all laughed, then Darcy left them to greet another customer.

Lisa paused a minute, thinking.

"What's the going rate for thoughts these days?"

Lisa looked up at Nick, who was leaning toward her across the table. "A quarter." She smiled. "Sorry, I spaced out there for a minute."

"It's been a busy day."

"Very." She took a sip of her drink. "I was thinking that whoever Del marries will be their aunt, too. I'll have to work on securing best-aunt-status before then."

She set her drink down then leaned forward herself, arms akimbo on the table. "So, what's next?"

"The best burger in Western Kentucky."

"I mean about the tunnels. Do you think there's more down there?" She looked up to see young Lily manhandling a tray holding Nick's shake as well as their burgers and loaded fries. "Well, here's your next step."

A minute later, with their burgers in front of them and Lily walking way, Nick reached his hand out. "Pray with me?"

Surprised, Lisa took his hand without thinking.

"Father, thank You for the day You've given us, and for the safety and provision You give us. Thank You for this food and for the hands that prepared it. In Your name, Amen."

Lisa whispered, "Amen." The topic of religion hadn't come up, and she supposed she should have known Nick had been brought up similarly to her, but you never knew. He squeezed her hand and smiled at her, then immediately turned his attention to his plate. He didn't waste any time. He dipped his fry into the "loaded" part of the dish. He leaned over the plate when the melted cheese, onion, and chili threatened to cover his shirt.

"Right?"

"So good." He closed his eyes, a rapt expression on his face.

Lisa laughed. "Told ya."

Her attention was diverted when she heard another "ding" of the bell on the door. Darcy was greeting another customer, the local sheriff.

But the sheriff wasn't looking at Darcy. He was looking at them.

17

Lisa groaned inwardly as Sheriff Clay Lacy approached their table. He removed his hat and smoothed his closely-cropped hair before he got to their table. What now?

"Lisa, Nick." Clay hitched his pants up a notch and cleared his throat.

"How are you, Clay?" She may as well be pleasant. After all, it wasn't completely his fault they'd had two disastrous dates. She could take some of the responsibility.

"Good. Good. Sorry to interrupt your lunch, but I was wondering, Nick, if we could talk sometime soon?"

Nick looked at Lisa. She shrugged her shoulders and took a bite of her burger. Clay seemed to dismiss her. It would seem that this wasn't her rodeo.

"Sure. After lunch okay? Two o'clock?"

Clay looked off and then back at Nick. "That'll be fine. You want to come by the office in town, or meet back at your property?"

"I'd be glad to see you in town. Anything wrong?"

"No, nothing's wrong. I need to go over a few things and hopefully we can get your property released soon."

"Great. Lisa's chomping at the bit to get started." Nick grinned at Lisa, then at Clay, who wasn't smiling.

Lisa noticed the irritated expression on her old acquaintance's face. Oh brother. He's jealous.

"I'm sure she is." He glanced at Lisa and then put his hat back on. "I'll leave you to your lunch, and see you at two." He walked away without as much as a goodbye.

"Interesting." Lisa couldn't hold it in. She started laughing.

"What's the deal with you two? Were you an item at one time?" Nick had waited a moment for her to stop laughing, but she still had a case of the giggles every time she thought she was finished.

"Oh, Nick. Don't *even* go there." Wiping the tears from her face, she shook her head emphatically. "I don't mean to be self-indulgent, but Clay has been asking me out on dates since fifth grade."

"And?"

"And in a fit of desperation, I said 'yes,' and he's never let go of it." She had said too much, already. It wasn't one of her finer moments, in her opinion.

Nick had finished his burger and was waiting as she ate each individual french fry with ketchup. Chin in hand, he smiled over at her. "We've all had those moments."

She snorted gracefully. "I'm sure you never had to worry about an emergency date in your life."

"Oh, you'd be surprised." He had lifted one eyebrow, and still had that smile on his face.

"I'd like to hear about that sometime." Was it getting warm in there?

"You first." Arms crossed, he leaned toward her, his eyes capturing hers.

She twisted her lips, skeptical. Once she had caught herself in the mirror making that exact face, and realized she resembled her grandmother when she did it. Funny how those thoughts came at weird times.

"It was senior prom."

"Ouch."

"What? I haven't even told you anything."

"Just the words 'senior prom' puts most guys in mind of elastic neckwear and fluffy dresses."

"Yeah." She sighed. "My dress was perfect. Mint green, beaded bodice and tulle skirt that literally had to be stuffed into the car when he picked me up."

"What did he drive?" His smile was getting mischievous.

"A 2000 P.T. Cruiser. His grandmother's hand-me-down car."

"Color?"

"Kind of a dirty gold. You never knew if it was clean or not." As she saw him start to laugh, she held up a finger. "I have to say, though, what it lacked in the 'coolness factor,' it makes up for in cargo capacity."

"How's that?" His eyebrow raised.

"He could haul four other football players and their gear."

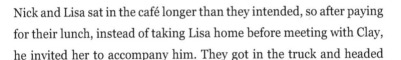

Nick and Lisa sat in the café longer than they intended, so after paying for their lunch, instead of taking Lisa home before meeting with Clay, he invited her to accompany him. They got in the truck and headed the ten miles toward Marion.

"But he didn't want me there, obviously."

"I would imagine because he can't handle being near you after your amazing prom date." He placed his hand on his heart and imitated a swoon.

"Very funny. I knew I'd regret telling you about it." She sighed. "The dress was never the same after that. Besides him stepping all over it, the punch he spilled on my dress and shoes was red. I had hoped to wear it for Class Night."

His eyebrows went down. "What does the color of the punch have to do with anything?"

She looked at him across the cab of the pickup. "Everyone knows red punch is impossible to get out of anything."

"Anything?"

"Yes. Even Scotchgard fabric protector doesn't guarantee against it."

"You're kidding."

"Nope. I'm an interior designer. I know stuff."

He laughed out loud, more relaxed than he should be on the way to meet the sheriff about an ongoing investigation on his property. "Yes, you do."

When they arrived and parked on the court square, Lisa stopped at Bowtanicals gift and decor shop. "I'll browse around in here. I need to shop for some stuff for Mel's nursery anyway, and Elliot called me when they got in new baby items that don't scream *baby*."

"Do things really 'scream'?"

"Yes. Trust me on this." She looked at her phone to check the time. "You better get over there. Clay is nothing if not prompt."

"More bad memories."

"You have no idea."

He shook his head and grinned. "Okay, I'll text you when I get out and find out where you are."

"Oh, I'll still be here. I haven't been in a while."

"Wish me luck?"

"No such thing. I'll pray for you." She winked absently and went into the store.

Nick's allowed his gaze to follow her, wondering if he had a goofy grin on his face. *Get over it, Nick, back to business.* He peered up at the 1960s-era courthouse, curious as to what he would find out from Clay.

No reason to wonder. All he had to do was go in and see if they could get on with this project. He'd love to be able to tell Lisa not only could they start the project, but they could also explore the rest of the cave where they had it marked off.

He climbed the stairs and looked left and right through the empty hallway. The only office with an open door and its lights on was the sheriff's office.

He entered to a tall counter on his left with the secretary/receptionist on the phone sporting two other blinking buttons beside the solid light of the line she was on. She held up a finger as a "wait a minute" signal, and he nodded.

In the meantime, before she could get off the phone from a citizen who, according the side of the conversation he could hear, had suspicions of young folk terrorizing his goats at night, Clay walked in from behind her and motioned for Nick to come through the opening and back to his office.

He gestured for him to sit in the mid-century vinyl-covered guest chair. Original to the building? "Thanks for coming in, Nick. Sorry to cut your lunch short."

"No problem. Lisa and I had been out to the tunnel to look around."

"Not the crime scene, I hope?" Clay glanced at him sharply.

"No, we steered clear of the house and went in from the river end."

"Yeah, the FBI made short work of that end of the tunnel. Seems there's more than one down there that meet."

"We almost got turned around at one point. We thought we were going south, but when I checked my compass, found out we were going east instead."

"Interesting. Special Agent Congdon told me they explored one tunnel heading west."

"I thought there was another one down there. I'll have to check that one out later." Nick took a deep breath. "In the meantime, what's the status of the part of the cellar keeping me from my project?"

Clay leaned forward and pushed a piece of paper across his desk, and Nick took it from him, then scanned the sheet to decipher the findings. "So, according to this, it seems as if they're done with the investigation?"

"Not completely, but enough that they'll let you back in your house." Clay reclined in his chair, which emanated a loud squeak from the aging mechanism. Nick wondered how many sheriffs the chair had served.

"So I can begin the renovation?" He wanted to get this straight before he got started and stopped yet again.

"Looks like it." The young sheriff regarded Nick, a slight frown on his face. "The FBI strongly suggested they be able to get in touch with you, should they need to come back at some point."

"Could I get his contact information? We found a desk with a journal in it, along with parts from an old still."

"Yeah, they told me about the still, but said it was as old as the skeleton they found."

"I'm surprised you didn't tell me about that." Nick felt his temper rising. *Keep it cool, Nick, no reason to get in bad with the local authorities.*

"Sorry. The body took precedence." Clay flipped through a folder he'd opened. "We're still working on identifying it. The victim is a male, approximately thirty-five years old, probably down there since the late sixties."

"Do you mean the 1960s?"

Clay looked at Nick and nodded. "Don't suppose anyone in your family would know about that?"

He thought before he spouted off that his family couldn't be involved. Could they? "I've never heard anything about the tunnel, so I wouldn't know." *But you can be sure I'm going to ask Dad if he knew about the tunnel system.*

"Didn't figure, but thought I'd ask." Clay closed the folder and looked across his desk. "You're free to do anything to your property you want, as long as it's legal."

What did he mean by that? "Good. I'm hoping to get a crew out there next week, then, and I should be with them most of the time. If I'm not, Lisa or my foreman will be there."

Clay didn't appear to be any happier about that. "Good. Just be careful." The brow furrowed even further. "I shouldn't tell you this, but since Lisa's involved in your project, I'll bend the rules."

Nick looked him in the eye. "What's going on, Clay?"

"I don't know if they meant me to hear this, but there was talk of a Mafia connection with the dead guy."

"Which one?"

Clay chuckled. "You do seem to have an overabundance of corpses on your property." He sobered. "The more recent one. His wallet was missing, but there was a security company ID card in his money belt, which was tough to get to with the decomposition."

Nick shook his head in disgust. "Mafia? As in, 'Godfather-Mafia?'"

Clay nodded and leaned forward, bringing his face closer to Nick's. "Out of Chicago. I can't say any more right now. If it gets back to them that you know any of this, I never said a word, understood?"

"Understood."

"It's just—"

"I get it. You want to protect Lisa." He leveled a gaze at the sheriff. "I do, too."

18

"Want to take a little trip to a creepy, smelly basement?"

Nick had found Lisa just as she'd said, still wandering around the boutique perusing various nursery and other decorative items.

Lisa put down the fluffy baby blanket she'd been squeezing and quirked an eyebrow at him. "Tell me that isn't your pick-up line, because if it is, I feel sorry for you."

"No, Clay told me they've cleared my property. I want to get a demo crew in there next week, so I want to go back to the room where we found the body. We haven't been back in there since the first day."

"I may wish I hadn't eaten those loaded fries." She wrinkled her nose. "But I'm game. Surely all the traffic down there has scared off any would-be criminals or ghosts."

"Ghosts?" He had seen her little shiver of apprehension.

"I know, I'm silly. I don't believe in ghosts, but..."

"Yeah, I know, 'but...'" He waited as she talked to the store clerk about holding a few items, then turned to leave. He held the door open for her. "Ladies first?"

She grinned as she hopped into the cab of the truck. "Thank you, kind sir. When we get to the house, I'll let you go first."

He walked around the front of the vehicle after shutting her door. After he'd buckled his seatbelt, he turned to her. "So you'll sacrifice me when the stakes are higher?"

"Definitely." She fastened her seat belt and settled in. "But you can be assured if anything gets you, I'll run for help."

"Noted." He pulled out of the parking space, onto Main Street, and turned left on 91 at one of two stoplights in town. He laughed and felt as if something had already "gotten" him. Namely one Lisa Reno.

The crime scene tape was still attached to the doorframe leading to the basement, and Lisa pulled it off and removed the residual tape before going down behind Nick. If possible, the basement seemed even dirtier and dingier than it had the first time Lisa had seen it.

"This is where it all started." Nick walked around, pulling the chains to turn on the various bare-bulb fixtures in the space.

Lisa placed the pet taxi on one of the abandoned appliances. She saw the moisture on the floor and chuckled. "Looks like you have one of those self-drying basements." She pointed to the crack.

"I remember when I was a kid, it would rain hard and the basement would get wet, and by the next day what water had seeped in through the cracks, had seeped out." He shrugged. "Beats getting the shop-vac out every time it rains."

"I hear you." She took a deep breath and walked over to the open door they had discovered on their first exploration of the house. "Ready to check this out?"

"Let's do this." He paused to check his flashlight, then turned to her. "I noticed you brought the cat carrier."

"Yes. Did you think Clay would rescue them and bring them to me?" The odds were nil. Clay never cared for animals much, which she had a hard time understanding.

Nick lifted an eyebrow. "What do you think?"

"Are you a mind reader?"

He laughed. "No, but I remember the look he gave you when you were more worried about the cats than the dead body in the basement."

"Hey, there was nothing I could do for that guy, but the cats? Plus, thinking about the cats took my mind off the grossness of the decomposing corpse in the basement." She gave him a wary grin. "Let's get in there and get it over with. I want to see if Fluffy and company are still around.

The room past the secret door was unchanged except for things that had been moved around where the search had taken place and fingerprint powder on surfaces. The door leading to the tunnel was standing open, darkness beckoning to them. She noticed the musty smell of dirt and the river. Big improvement on their last exploration of the space.

"Did you bring a bigger flashlight this time?" She found the flashlight app on her phone, but it wasn't as bright as she wanted.

Nick reached into the bag he carried and pulled out his Maglite. "This big enough?"

"My favorite. The four-battery kind."

He nodded. "Makes a good weapon, too."

"Are you expecting trouble?"

"No, but I wished for it when we found the dead guy down here. I wasn't sure what we were walking into."

Nick illuminated the room where they had been surprised by a corpse a few weeks ago. He pointed to the dark stain on the aged concrete floor. "Here's the scene of the crime."

Lisa felt a shiver run through her veins and went out of her way to walk around it.

Nick chuckled. "It's dry."

"I know, but it's similar to walking over a grave in the graveyard. I know they're not really there, but it's still creepy." She shrugged her shoulders and pulled out her phone and its flashlight to illuminate the other side of the room.

A rustling sound got her attention. Rats? Mice? With a small but fierce yowl, a tiny ball of fur leapt out of the corner and put its needle-sharp claws into the backside of Nick's leg.

"Whoa!"

Lisa couldn't help it. When Nick yelled in surprise, she started laughing. "You've been attacked!"

He turned to see the calico kitten glaring up at him, frustrated at trying to detach herself from Nick's jeans, but with no luck. "Hey, little girl." He gently pulled on the kitten's body, her plump little tummy filling his hand nicely. "Let's get you loose and find your family, okay?"

"Glad it wasn't a rat." Lisa grinned when he handed the kitten to her. It immediately snuggled up under her chin. "Oh no."

"What?" Nick looked surprised.

"She likes me."

"Why is that an 'oh no' statement?"

"Because I already have cats." She gave him a half smile. "As in multiple"

He picked up the first kitten's brother, a solid black with a white star on his chest, kicking his tiny feet wildly as he yelled for his mama. He turned it to look it in the eyes. "Hey, bud. I'm here to rescue you. Got it?"

"I don't think they care. They seem to be doing well for themselves."

"Yeah, well my basement is not a good place for indoor-outdoor cats. Maybe the barn?"

"That could work, at least while construction is going on. What about later, though?" Lisa chewed her bottom lip. She didn't want to think about the cats being abandoned when the work was done and Nick decided to sell the place.

But maybe he wouldn't. Maybe he would decide to stay.

"I say we set them up in the barn for now. Maybe they'll keep the mouse population down." He glanced at her. "We'll let tomorrow take care of itself."

19

Now that local law enforcement had released Nick's property for them to work, the real planning could begin. The demolition crew was working with Nick today, and Lisa knew he had ordered a couple of loads of gravel to reinforce the driveway for the extra truck traffic in and out during construction.

At her desk, Lisa chewed her bottom lip as she scanned the floorplan, making note of questions she needed to be sure to ask Nick. She wanted to check on the crew removing the aged vinyl siding and make sure they could get the outside, or envelope, of the house secured before the fall rainy season began.

The journal she and Nick found in the tunnel sat there, on the corner of her desk, beckoning her to snoop. She should wait for Nick. But it was drawing her, enticing her to explore the hidden secrets it held, and since she was at a standstill until the siding was off the house, why not peruse it now?

The entry they found while still underground was from 1924, but they hadn't started at the beginning. She laid the volume carefully on her desk and turned to the first page, which was dated June, 1921. In the beginning, it read like a simple diary of the daily tasks of a farm wife. Weather report, garden progress, et cetera. When she turned to the last entry, dated August 1935, it was much different.

She thought a minute. Crittenden County had been a dry county from the time of Prohibition—the eighteenth amendment—until the past year, when it became legal to purchase package liquor in stores and by-the-drink liquor in restaurants. In 1935, the federal Prohibition amendment had been repealed–but not here.

She scanned through it, trying to find where it changed. Here. The handwriting became more masculine in about 1933. Flipping back a few pages, she caught her breath. She had to show this to Nick. It would take reading it cover to cover to get the entire story, but he needed to know more about his family's history.

A horn honked outside and her head came up at the sound. A grin spread across her face as she saw Del hoist himself out of his pickup truck and onto crutches. Physical therapy had been good for him, and he'd have more when he got his foot out of the protective boot he was stuck with for another few weeks.

She rushed over to the door to open it for him. "This is a surprise. What are you doing here?"

"I decided since my left foot is the one in the boot, nothing is stopping me from making short drives."

"Did you get permission?" She gave him a look, encouraging him to tell the truth.

"From whom?" He winked. "See, my English degree isn't wasted."

"You're a riot." She shook her head and narrowed her eyes. "From the doctor."

"Well, the therapist said he didn't see anything wrong with me driving short distances as long as I didn't try driving as far as Paducah or Evansville." He snorted. "So I'll still have to be chauffeured to the doctor at the Orthopedic Institute next week."

"Not a problem. I would have taken you to therapy today."

"I know. I thought it would be easier to drive there and ask forgiveness instead of permission. That's why I didn't tell you what time I had to be there."

"Figures."

"I'm hoping I can get this thing off next week." He lowered himself into the chair next to her desk. "The therapist seemed to think maybe I would."

"I hope he didn't get your hopes up for nothing."

"We're thinking positively, dear sister." He turned and saw the blueprint she'd been studying. "Let me see."

She turned the plan sideways.

"This looks good." He studied the plan closely. Lisa could see the wheels turning in his brain, calculating different costs and troubleshooting. He shot her a look. "Keeping the plaster?"

She nodded. "Planning on it. There will be lots and lots of holes to patch. Think you'll be up to it?"

"Hope so. There's something infinitely satisfying about plaster-work."

"I'm glad you think so. Personally, I hate it."

"You don't like to cut in the corners and trim when you paint, either." He grinned. "Patience, little one."

"You seem to enjoy it, so I let you take care of it. Give me a paint sprayer or roller any day."

"Have you talked to the electrician yet?" He didn't look up as he studied the plan. "I noticed the last time the box was updated, it had a mixture of breakers and knob-and-tube."

She waved her hand. "All that has to go. A three thousand-square-foot house needs more than a hundred-amp breaker panel. We'll be starting from scratch as much as possible."

"Good. I know Nick is used to new construction." Del arched an eyebrow at her.

"He is, but he's starting to come over to the light, restoration-wise."

"I hope so. If I remember correctly, it had nice plaster trim in places."

Lisa nodded. "Some of it was damaged with a roof leak, but I'll let you decide what's salvageable."

"Sounds like a plan." He pulled himself back up. "Are you hungry?"

"I could eat. What do you have in mind?"

Del's stomach grumbled and they both laughed. He rubbed his belly. "I've got a hankering for a double-cheese burger and loaded fries."

Lisa gave him a grin. "And maybe chocolate pie?"

"The sky's the limit. I'll take my chocolate in shake form."

"If the sky's the limit, does this mean lunch is on you?" She gathered her purse and checked to make sure she had her keys.

"Yep. As much as you've done for me lately, I can never buy enough chocolate pie to thank you."

"No, you can't." She grinned. "I'm meeting Nick at the house this afternoon." She locked the door as they exited, then rushed to get to the passenger side door ahead of Del.

"No, he's meeting us at the café." This time he had both eyebrows going.

"What's the eyebrow thing supposed to mean?" She felt her heart beat a little faster.

"Whatever you want it to, little sister. Whatever you want it to."

She swatted his arm and opened the truck door for him. "Chivalry is dead."

"Hey, don't mess with the afflicted, especially when they're buying lunch." He eased himself into the driver's seat and stowed his crutches behind him in the crew cab.

Lisa buckled up and shook her head. "You've been afflicted all your life."

"Can't argue with you there."

Nick looked at his phone to check the time. He'd told his foreman he'd be back by one thirty, but if Del and Lisa didn't show up soon, he'd have to order without them. When the bell on the door sent out a shrill ding, he smiled when he saw Lisa striding in, Del behind her on crutches. He stood up.

"Hey, I was beginning to think you'd ditched me."

He could tell Lisa was excited. Was she that happy to see him?

Del took the seat across from Nick, between him and Lisa propping his crutches up as he scooted his chair.

"Nick, I found something..." He pulled out the chair for her and she sat. "I found something in the journal."

"Interesting?"

"Very." She lifted her eyebrows to continue.

"Here, let me take those and put them out of the way, 'kay?" Darcy had rushed over as soon as her stepbrother and stepsister had entered. She leaned the crutches in the corner close to their table, a little breathless when she returned. "Y'all doing all right today?"

Nick grinned. Del's face was as red as a beet, about like Darcy's. Lisa popped up out of her chair and hugged the slight blonde, and answered the question. "We're doing great."

"I see you finally got the hermit out of his cave." Darcy sent Del a teasing look, which was returned with a goofy grin.

"I'm cleared to drive, so you may be seeing more of me." Del took the menu and grinned some more. Nick thought his buddy was a little smitten.

"I won't complain about that." Darcy handed out the other two menus. "Can I get y'all something to drink?"

"I'll have water with lemon, please." Lisa looked up. "Oh, and Dad called the other day. Sounds like they're enjoying the cruise from Alaska to Seattle."

"Mom's been sending me pictures. Want me to send them to you? They're amazing."

"I'd love to see them. Dad asks questions about the business, so I learn more about the trip from what you hear from Roxy than I do from Dad." She laughed.

"Nick? Del?"

Nick caught Lisa's smile. She seemed glad he was there.

"Drink? I'll have a sweet tea, please, no lemon."

"Noted." She stood a second. "Del?"

"Sweet tea with lemon." He shrugged and patted his stomach. "I decided to lay off the milkshakes."

"Probably a good idea."

"Hey, now. What's that supposed to mean?"

Darcy twisted her lips in an expression between a laugh and a smile. "All this inactivity can't be good for you. You're not getting any younger, you know."

Del snorted in surprise. "I'll have you know I weigh the same as I did when I graduated from college."

"I'm sure you do, and male metabolism has always been a mystery to me." Darcy chuckled. "I'll let you look at the menu, and be back in a minute."

"Thanks, Darcy." Nick laughed. "She got to you, man."

Del shifted in his seat. "Maybe I am losing a little muscle tone."

Lisa hid her face behind the menu, but Nick saw her hands shake with laughter.

"I'll get back in shape as soon as this leg is healed up."

Nick nodded, not meeting his eyes for fear of laughter. "I'm sure you will."

"I'll lay off the sodas. They say by doing that you can lose ten pounds." Del huffed a little.

Lisa laid down her menu and ignored her brother. "I think I'm getting the grilled meatloaf sandwich and homemade potato chips. How about you, Nick?"

"That sounds good. But I'm going for the pork tenderloin sandwich and corn nuggets. Those things are amazing." He glanced over at a frowning Del. "How about you?"

"I'm looking over the 'healthy eating' options."

Lisa burst out laughing. "As long as you remember you owe me a piece of chocolate pie."

"I'll at least be able to smell it." Del tossed the menu down. "I'll have the chef's salad with Ranch dressing."

20

Lead and asbestos abated, Lisa surveyed the pockmarked plaster walls and paper-covered hardwood floors as she swiped a piece of sawdust from her nose. The sound of vinyl siding being ripped off was the sound of progress. On the inside, demolition had been done in the area where they wanted to open it up, and the structural engineer had come out to check it.

Of course, it was load bearing, so a laminated beam had been ordered yesterday. Until then, that particular wall was bare of plaster and the knob-and-tube wiring was exposed. Every electrician's nightmare began with that stuff.

The easy way to do it would be to take down all the plaster, but neither she nor Nick wanted get rid of it. Plaster was good for sound-proofing, fire-proofing, and generally made a house more substantial. Fortunately, she had a good plaster guy. She twisted her lips in a frown. Unfortunately, he had a broken leg. She could only hope Del's leg would be healed sufficiently by the time they were ready for that step. She made a note to check with Nick for a backup plaster contractor.

Back in what would be the kitchen, Lisa had her checklist in hand and was jotting down ideas when she heard a truck pull up in the recently graveled front drive. She walked through the dining room and then the living room, where she could see out the wavy glass of the original windows and smiled. Nick was here. He had stopped by the lumber supply company after lunch, and Del had taken her back to the office to get her truck.

"Honey, I'm home." Nick's chuckle made her smile and she felt the heat rush to her face.

"Cute." She shook her head at him as they met in the doorway between the dining room and living room.

He put his hands in his pockets and stood there, staring at her. Suddenly he pulled his hand out and reached for her. No, not for her, for something in her hair. "Hold still."

"What is it?" It could be anything. Spider? Cobweb?"

"Piece of fiber from the plaster. There. Got it."

"I was afraid it was a spider." She reddened and touched the area of her head where his hand had been.

He grinned. "I thought it was, at first." He held his hand out to show her the grungy bit of debris. "Genuine antique horsehair."

"Gross, but cool."

"You were telling me about the journal, but we got sidetracked."

"Yes! I looked through it this morning, and it dates from 1920 to 1935. Your great-grandmother's writing is in it through 1933, then the writing changes."

"That's about the time she died. I always heard she died fairly young."

Lisa studied him thoughtfully. "Did you ever hear how she died?"

"No, I figured it was something that killed lots of people back then—germs, flu, infection. You name it, it killed people."

"I was curious, so I went back a few pages from when her writing stopped, and while it was her writing, it was a little different. No more garden reports, but more of an actual diary." She frowned. "She wasn't well, but she didn't know what was wrong. She seemed worried about her son, and talked about strangers that made her afraid to be in her own house."

Nick pondered this information. "Did she say who these strangers were?"

"No, but past this point there were a few pages torn out. Strange. Right after that, it went back to reports of liquor sales and weather reports."

"I'll go through Gran's genealogy info. I have it at my house. It records the birth and death dates, but she had some copies of things she'd found along the way. Maybe there's something there that would answer these questions."

She nodded "Speaking of old stuff..."

Tossing the bit of horsehair debris to the floor, he scanned around at the cleaner workspace. "Looks a lot different with the wall nearly down."

"I can't wait to see it when the beam goes up." Lisa smiled, getting the image in her mind of what it could be.

He nodded. "When will it get here?"

She glanced down at her list. "Middle of next week. Your guys will have the siding off in another couple of days."

"They could be ready tomorrow if you are." Eyebrows raised, he seemed excited. "I'm ready to get this thing started."

"I know. One step forward, ten steps back, seems like." She checked her list again. "Have you decided on the windows?"

"You're going to think I'm crazy." He looked around at the multitude of wooden, original windows. "Which would be about right, because I think I'm crazy, too." He took a deep breath and gave her a sidelong glance. "I'm going to restore them."

Happiness bubbled up inside her. "All of them? Are you serious?"

"Yes, all of them." He raised his hands as if to ward off objection. "I know, it'll extend the timeline exponentially, but I want to keep the character alive."

She didn't hesitate. Lisa went for it and threw herself into his arms and gave him a fierce hug. "You don't know how happy you've made me."

He began to laugh and tightened his arms around her, hugging her back.

When it lingered a hair past decorum, Lisa realized she had instigated the hug. Face so hot she felt it would burst into flames, she drew back and glanced up into his face. "Sorry. I lost my head there for a minute."

"I'm not complaining."

Why did she feel so right in his arms? The impulsive hug she gave him over windows, of all things, shook him more than he felt warranted. If it had lasted a few seconds longer...

He cleared his throat. Don't go there. Not worth it.

She seemed to hesitate, too. After avoiding his eyes for what felt like an eternity, she peeked up and then away again. "So we're going to restore the windows? I'm so excited! Nobody wants to do that except the die-hard restoration nuts." She opened her eyes wider and drew in her breath. "Are you a convert?"

He cut his eyes to the side, slightly embarrassed. "I'll admit it. I've been reading restoration blogs. There's this one guy out of Florida that makes a great case for restoration instead of replacement."

"I know the one. He's pretty convincing."

"Do you have a window guy?"

"Or gal?" She tilted her head and put her hand on her hip, which only served to make him smile again.

"Okay, window person?"

"As a matter of fact, I do. You realize we have an extensive Amish community in this neighborhood? Some amazing craftsmen live close by. We've contracted with them before. We have one gentleman who loves to get his hands on old wood, and this house would be right up his alley."

"Perfect. Can I go with you to talk to him?" He watched as she wrote down the name and address. "I'm assuming he doesn't have a phone."

"He shares one with two other businesses, but going out there would be the best way to catch him."

He glanced down at his watch. There were a million things he could be doing, but he'd already talked himself out of them. He raised an eyebrow at her. "Road trip?"

She snorted. "If by road trip you mean driving down Cotton Patch Road about a half a mile."

"Whatever it takes. From what I remember, the road's so curvy you meet yourself coming."

"It is, and the bridge is out from all the rain early this year, so be glad Enoch is on this side of it or we would be taking a road trip." She put her portfolio with her list into her bag and placed the straps on her shoulder. "Ready?"

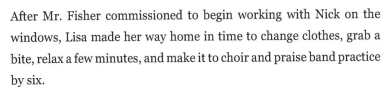

After Mr. Fisher commissioned to begin working with Nick on the windows, Lisa made her way home in time to change clothes, grab a bite, relax a few minutes, and make it to choir and praise band practice by six.

She stayed busy, and sometimes she regretted she didn't have more of a social life outside of the church. She'd been brought up to serve in her local church, and except for the months after Mom's illness and death, Dad was a great example of a man who loved his church.

She loved it, but maybe she was a little burned out. Keyboardists were getting fewer and farther between, so she was often on call for both choir and band, like tonight.

The aroma of her baking frozen pizza enticing her, she pulled a fresh shirt over her head and padded, barefoot, into the kitchen to take it out of the oven. Four-cheese. Her favorite.

She found herself, plate and glass in hand, heading to her small living room where she had a club chair and ottoman calling her name. It was "her chair." If she wasn't in it, one of her cats claimed it. She nudged Jack out of the chair and he went, unwillingly. "Sorry bud, but this is my only shot at sitting for more than five minutes."

Flipping through the channels, she landed on a reality show with young girls vying to be the next supermodel. *Bless their hearts. Nope.* A few channels further, and she had the Home channel, and there was her old show. She missed it.

She muted the sound for a minute to bless her food. Taking a deep breath, she prayed. "Lord, thank You for this food, and Your watch-care today. Be with Del, and Dad and Roxy, and keep them all safe and well." She paused. "And God, can I complain a little bit?" She opened her eyes and lifted them to the ceiling as if God wasn't everywhere all at once anyway. "I'm tired, and I'm lonely, and out of sorts. Maybe I just miss Dad, and with Del recuperating, I miss having him to work with. Thank You for sending Nick, and for his being a kindred spirit." Should she ask? Dared she?

"Um, Father, would there be any chance...?" She shook her head. "I know, surely he would have said something by now. I'm sorry. I leave it all in Your hands, and then try to take it up again." Tears smarted in her eyes. "Thank You for being there, God. Amen."

She looked up in time to see the third run-down house her former employers were showing a family. Even from here, she could tell it would be more than a simple fixer-upper. More like a "tearer-downer." Her anxiety decreased as she watched the familiar program. She could have gone back to Texas and taken up where she left off two years ago.

Michael was still with them, and they had been in contact with her as recently as last fall. Could she drop right back in as if nothing had happened? Maybe she should consider it. Dad had Roxy now, and Del needed to find his own partner.

The more she thought about it, the more she considered the idea of leaving and starting over somewhere else. She loved her hometown. There was no place like it. But how would she ever meet anyone here? There were the same people she'd known all her life, and maybe it wasn't healthy to be so insular.

Would leaving everything she knew solve her problem? Maybe. Maybe not. She took a deep breath and looked down at the cat jumping up to her lap as soon as she laid aside her plate. Jack made sure she knew he was around. He made sure to put his head directly under her hand so she would know to scratch him behind the ears. He had her trained to do what pleased him.

Maybe she should be more like Jack.

21

Nick smiled at the sheriff's office manager and nodded when she waved him through to Clay Lacey's office. Again on the phone, from what he could hear, it sounded like this time there had been an ATV stolen along with vandalism to a garage on a farm out in the county.

Clay looked up from the papers on his desk. "Hi Nick, glad you could come in. Thought I would give you an update on what's been going on with the evidence found in your house."

Nick sat on the ancient green vinyl side chair across from the sheriff's desk. "Great. What's the latest?"

"The FBI had the body transferred to their lab at Quantico when they found evidence tying it to money laundering across state lines."

"Did they identify it?" Nick wondered how much more convoluted this situation could get. "I got the idea that last time we talked, they had ID'd him."

Clay nodded. "They had, but they weren't ready to divulge it. It's looking like a drug deal gone wrong." Clay paused, sorting through papers. "The dead guy was a Lonnie March, from Chicago. They found evidence further into the tunnel of drug dealing. Not manufacturing, but evidence points to someone using the tunnels as a way station for dealers to pick up drugs and drop off money, and vice-versa."

"Did they narrow down the time of death?" Surely they had, or Clay wouldn't be so free with his information.

"Looks like it was further back than we thought. The cool damp of the tunnel slowed decomp, so it was more like February or March when he was killed. They also found a missing-person report from the south side of Chicago for the guy, dated March twenty-fifth."

"That's before I bought the place."

"I know. That's why I wanted to let you know you're off the 'person of interest' list unless something else comes up. Of course, that includes Lisa and Del Reno, as well."

Nick took a deep breath. "Thanks, Clay. I appreciate the information. Out of curiosity, do they have any idea who may have killed him?"

"Not a clue. They're still testing all the evidence, so there will be more results from time to time."

"What about the skeletal remains? Any ideas?"

Clay frowned and leaned forward. "That's something else I wanted to talk to you about."

That sounded ominous. "Okay. What do you know?"

"Of course it was completely down to the skeleton, and animals had dragged it around some, scattering the bones and other evidence."

I didn't want to know that. "Was there anything around it to identify it?"

"According to the pathologists in Madisonville, it was a male, approximately thirty-five years old, and looking at the clothing and the gun, looks like it happened in the late 1960s."

"That's what you told me when it was first found." That would have been when his grandparents lived there. Dad would have been a small boy at the time. Surely...

"Right." Clay nodded, watching Nick closely.

Nick frowned. "Are they sure?"

"I'm afraid so."

"Any thoughts of DNA testing?"

"Not unless they have a good reason to do so. DNA wasn't used back then, but they may be able to get some from the bone marrow, or if there are some hair samples left with the follicle still attached."

Nick stood up. How could this have happened below his grandparents' property and they not know anything about it? Did they? Did Dad have any clue what was going on?

Lisa was up on a ladder, not her favorite place to be, chipping away at the paint holding the antique light fixture in place. The demo crew had left for the day, and besides, she didn't trust them to preserve it the way she wanted it done.

It had to be a hundred and ten degrees up close to the ceiling. What she wouldn't give for a powerful fan.

She almost had it. She scored the decades of paint sealing it to the ceiling, and had the small pry bar between the fixture and the plaster, ready to use physics and a lever to do what she wouldn't be able to do without the proper tools. She pushed down on the handle and heard it start to give. *Just not all at once, please...*

She felt the sudden weight of the fixture. Momentum had her falling about the time she heard a noise distracting her further.

"Lisa!"

As she lost control of the fixture and the ladder, her brain registered that it was Nick and he could help. "Catch the light fixture!"

Right before she hit the ground, she felt strong arms catch her and heard the fixture hit the floor.

"You were kidding, right?" Nick held her for a moment and then set her on her feet.

She scrutinized the heavy fixture and bit her lip. "Oh, I hope it's okay."

"You're welcome." He looked angry.

She felt her face heat up. "Thank you for rescuing me. But I'm more concerned about the fixture."

"That?" He picked it up and inspected it. "I think it would take a car crusher to hurt this thing." He put it down and flexed his arm.

"Yeah. It's pretty heavy, isn't it?"

"You thought you could get down an eight-foot ladder carrying this thing?" He glowered at her. "It weighs more than you do."

"It's original to the house. I want to rewire it and use it somewhere." Lisa walked over to it and pulled on the chain. When it didn't budge from the floor, she looked at him with wide eyes. "You weren't kidding." With both hands, she could lift it. Barely.

He shook his head and put his hands on his hips. "Where do you want it?"

"In the back of the Explorer?" She scrunched her nose. That technique usually worked to get Dad or Del to do the heavy lifting.

He hoisted it up from the base. "You know this thing is solid brass, don't you?"

"Yes, I know. I plan to strip the paint off of it and polish it up. You wait and see. It'll be beautiful." Mr. New-Construction would see what restoration really meant. She lifted her chin and stretched to her full height. "It would be a shame to lose this. Most houses don't still have old fixtures in them." She picked up a light-switch plate and showed him. "I'm also searching for push-button light switches to replace the old ones, so I can reuse the old brass switch plates."

She gave him her best smile and felt herself wilt a little bit at his dour expression.

"Could you please open the hatch of your truck so I can put this thing down?"

"Oh..." She grabbed her key fob and pushed the button in the direction of the vehicle, then watched as the hatch lifted. "Sorry. I tend to get carried away."

"That's okay. Get the door, please?" He shifted the weight to keep hold of the gargantuan load.

Lisa rushed to the door. "Watch the hole in the porch floor."

His eyebrow rose. "That's usually my line."

"Haha." She twisted her lips to keep from smiling, then watched as he easily carried the load and deposited it in her cargo space, hit the button to close the hatch and walk back to the porch. "Thanks."

"Why didn't you wait until I or one of the guys could help you?"

She shrugged her shoulders. "I don't know. For some reason, I always think I should at least try to do a task alone before asking for help. I knew it would be heavy, but it was up there so tight..." She knew she was avoiding his eyes. She'd not seen this side of him. The angry, frustrated side.

"That's because paint was holding it up there from a hundred years of the stuff."

"Anyway, what's done is done, and you were here at the right time."

He shook his head. "One of these days you're going to bite off more than you can chew."

She could only hope her perturbed sigh didn't tip him off to the fact that she'd heard that many times in her life. Maybe she could be a little reckless, but it would only hurt herself, wouldn't it? Del falls off a ladder and breaks his leg and nobody says anything about him being a klutz. Just part of the job.

"Are you okay?" He was staring at her with a frown.

"Sorry." She turned to go into the kitchen. She could ask him the same thing. As it stood, she was in no mood to get into this conversation. "Want some water?"

"Sure." He followed her through the entry to the kitchen. As he passed, he put his hand on the wall and looked up at the ceiling where the new beam held the upstairs in place. "Hard to believe there used to be a wall here. It should have always been this way."

"What have you been up to this afternoon? The crew thought you'd be back before they left." She handed him a cold bottle out of the cooler and turned a five-gallon bucket over to sit on. After a long and refreshing drink from her own bottle, she realized her tank top was soaked with sweat from her foray up the ladder. She was a hot mess. Literally. Her "messy bun" had to look worse than it had that morning.

"I planned to be back, but Clay called and wanted me to come by his office."

After another drag from her bottle, she quirked an eyebrow at him. "Has he found another crime he can pin on one of us?"

He grinned. Maybe he was relaxing a little bit. "No, he wanted to update me on what they found out from the bodies found on my property."

"Ouch. I hadn't really thought of that. Knowing this was the scene of murder and mayhem might keep you from wanting anything to do with this place."

He shook his head.. "No, but it is making me curious about my own family."

"How's that?"

"The skeletal remains? They've established he more than likely died in the late 1960s."

She thought a minute. Her parents were both born in the early sixties. "Was this the house your dad grew up in?"

"They moved here in 1964, when Dad was two, so it's the first house he remembers..." His expression changed. "I don't want to think that my grandmother and granddad were involved in whatever was going on."

What could she say? This was a blow. "Have you asked your dad about it?"

He raked his hand over his face and shook his head, then pushed back the hair that inevitably fell in his face. "Not yet."

"What about the newer one?"

"You mean the one we almost tripped over?" He gave her a half smile. "It seems that Mr. Lonnie March of Chicago was involved in drug dealing and was reported missing March twenty-fifth of this year. The medical examiner decided the date of death was further back than they first thought since he was in a cool, dark place."

"Lots of sins can be hidden in the dark. Including a corpse." She took a deep breath. "I don't know what they used, but the cleaning crew you hired to get rid of the smell was amazing."

"Detective Reed gave me the contact information for them. No amount of bleach could have gotten rid of the odor permeating the house."

"And us." She reached out and touched his hands, clasped together as he leaned his elbows on his knees.

He looked up and grinned at her, and turned his hands to grasp hers. She stared into his eyes, trying to sense what he was thinking and feeling. He was sad. Angry. Nobody to share these things with. Not sure what his dad remembered, or heard. Uncertain about the past, present, and future.

A little uncertain about her.

She knew the feeling.

22

After Lisa left, Nick sat on the front porch steps until the sun began to dip. He could see one star—probably a planet—and the colors were amazing. Surely sitting in so much beauty and serenity would still his heart. Surely the sight would take the edge off the roller coaster of emotions he'd felt today. But it didn't.

He knew alcohol wouldn't tame the monster inside. He'd tried that after Kristy and the baby...all it did was make him worthless on the job. Construction is unforgiving when you're not in top form.

Be Still.

Can't get much more still than a front porch in the boonies of Western Kentucky.

Be still and know.

Know? All he knew was he was tired of being sad, lonely, and angry. It was easy to hide it, most of the time, but he'd almost let it slip with Lisa today.

Be still and know that I am God.

Nick closed his eyes in pain. "I know You're here." He sat there, not moving. In his heart, he was raging. "Why?" He sat there a few more minutes, then got up and started walking back and forth in front of the house.

Finally, he gazed up and saw more stars, heard the crickets chirp and frogs croak, and decided he'd had enough. He shouted. "I don't want to live like this anymore. Do You hear me?"

Among the stars he viewed, he saw one veer off course and burn out. People related a shooting star to a message from God. It wasn't, and he knew it. But it got his attention anyway.

"Why would You give me success in my work and take Kristy away?" He closed his eyes to stop the tears threatening to flow. "And my baby. I don't know if it was a son or daughter."

The pain in his chest made him want to scream, but he didn't. Instead, he locked the house up, got in his truck, and spun out in the fresh gravel as he rushed down the lane. He was running, and if he hadn't had a dog that would miss him, he would have gotten on the interstate highway and kept driving.

The thirty-minute drive back to Kuttawa gave him time to roll down the windows and let the hot wind blow some sense back into him. No radio, no audio. Bits of scripture came to him.

I will never leave you nor forsake you...

Be anxious for nothing...

Come to me, all you who labor and are heavy laden, and I will give you rest...

And God will wipe away every tear from their eyes...

Nick wouldn't wait until Mom called. He needed information, and Dad was the only resource he had.

"Hello? Nick? Is that you?" Mom kept talking and didn't give him time to affirm her guesses.

"Hi, Mom. Are you busy?" He let Minnie out into the backyard. It was the same drill, every day. Minnie jumped and barked with excitement until he let her out. You'd think after being crated all day she'd run straight out to do her business, but no. She ran straight to her water dish. After that came the process of sniffing out every corner of the yard to make sure no renegade vermin had crossed his property since she last walked guard duty. She had a special love-hate relationship with birds.

"Dad's outside on the patio. Want me to get him for you?"

"Please. You can listen in, too." He could hear her opening the French doors leading to the patio and calling to Dad.

"Nick's on the phone."

"You know you could call his phone." There was a tinge of reproach in her voice. "Not that I'm not always happy to hear your voice, sweetie." Always a qualifier.

"I know. Your number is on the top of the list, so it's easier to hit yours." Maybe she bought it.

"Hang on and I'll put you on speaker." He waited, knowing she was settling into a chair, then adjusting her bifocals to find the Speaker button. "Are you still there?"

"I'm here, Mom. Hi, Dad. How are you?"

"'Bout like usual. What do you need?" Straight to the point.

Nick paused a second, trying to put the words together. He heard Dad sigh, sensed his impatience, and decided to go for it. "Did I tell you they found a second body down in those tunnels?"

"Yeah. What did they find out about it?"

"They're dating it back to the late sixties."

Dad was quiet. "Late sixties, you say?"

"Yep." Silence on the other end.

"Nick, how did the man die?" Mom came back on and sounded nervous as if she were covering for Dad.

"He was shot. There was a gun lying next to him, so no way to know if someone shot him, or if he shot himself." Was his dad thinking what he was thinking? Was there more drama in the family than either of them knew about?

"Any way to identify it?" Dad sounded emotional, which was out of character for him.

"It's skeletal remains. The sheriff said they might be able to do DNA testing, but since it's so old, they won't unless it's requested."

"Request it." The gruffness in Dad's voice was unmistakable.

"Come again?"

"Just do it. Request the test."

Nick needed more information if he was going to start digging around. "Is there something you're not telling me?" He could hear Dad whispering to Mom as his chair scraped the concrete surface.

"Nick, is it okay if your dad and I come up to the house tomorrow?" Mom sounded nervous, too. "We need to talk."

23

The emotional dam broke, and Dan Woodward stared at his son, eyes wide and rimmed red. "Mama could never reconcile that he was gone, even when Grandpa told her he'd found the boat overturned in the river."

Nick couldn't stop staring at his dad. This was the man who remained distant, gruff, even, any time he hinted at getting close at a deeper level. When his daughter-in-law was killed, he had hugged his son, but couldn't quite grieve with him. Stoic was the only word to describe him. Nick had always wondered why.

"So, Granddad wasn't my grandfather?" He was still trying to wrap his head around a lifetime of memories.

Dad hung his head and shook it, his shoulders slumped. "He and my mother married when I was ten. She refused to even see anyone until she reconciled with herself that my dad wasn't coming back. I barely remember him, but I was old enough to know Mac wasn't my dad. I wasn't very nice to him, and he tried. He really did."

Nick sat there, thinking, looking toward the house that held so many wonderful memories for himself, and so many hurtful ones for his dad. He and his parents sat on the old glider and rocker still occupying the space under the tree in the front yard. The porch was currently being torn out and replaced.

He stared at Dad, shifting his jaw as he tried to put words together. "Why did you never tell me Granddad was your stepfather?"

Dad took a deep breath and straightened in the rocker. "I thought it was best."

"Now he's not so sure," Mom spoke up, finally. She'd been quiet for an inordinate amount of time. "I tried to get him to talk to you about it, especially when Mac died, but he felt it was better to avoid the situation than to be forthright with his son." She wiped tears from her eyes and gave her husband a look of reproach.

"Granny never said anything, either." Nick shook his head, trying to clear it.

"I told her not to. Better, I thought, to let you think me and my dad didn't get along than learn my father was involved in rum-running."

That was new. "You mean to tell me..."

Dan Woodward gave his son a hard, but somehow sad, look. "Yes, my father and my grandfather were both involved with selling illegal liquor to a crime family in Chicago." He looked away, shaking his head, then back at Nick. "That's why you need to see if they can identify the body."

"You think your father may have committed suicide?"

"That, or my grandfather or someone in the mob family killed him. There's may be no way to know, exactly, but if it's Daniel Woodward, Sr., I need to know it and be able to bury him next to Mom." He took a long look at the house where he grew up. "I got out of here as soon as I could. It hurt Mom, but I figured she had Mac, so she'd made her choice."

"How—?"

"How could I do that to my mother?" Dad snorted. "When you're eighteen and idolize your grandfather, you're stupid enough to make those choices."

"What was he like?"

"Grandpa?" He thought a minute and smiled. "Zebulon Woodward was big, boisterous, and never met a stranger." Sadness crossed his face. "He taught me how to fish, how to hammer a nail straight, and how to ask a girl out on a date. He was a deacon in the church, and I never knew about his illegal activities until long after he died."

"How old were you when he passed?"

"I was eight years old. I had no memories of my father, and when Mac came along, I'd been two years without Grandpa, as well. I was one angry little boy." He glanced up at his son. "Everyone said I took after him, and they were right. He was angry, too."

Nick sat there, waiting. Hoping for answers, but not expecting any. How did his dad overcome the anger? More importantly, do you ever?

"As you get older, you try to forget, but you never really do. For a long time, I thought the world owed me something. When I met your mom, she got me back to church, and I met Jesus."

"It's not a magic bullet." Mom reached over for his dad's hand and squeezed it. "We had our ups and downs, and your dad has never been forthcoming about his feelings. It took a lot of healing to get to this point."

Nick sat there, staring toward the house. He didn't want to look at either of them. "I'm not sure what to say about all this."

"I'm sorry, son. I truly am. I've let the lie I perpetuated come between us." Dad cleared his throat and stood, stuffing his hands in his pockets. "I've got a lot more of my grandpa in me than my dad or stepdad, and I think that's one reason Mom left me alone when I decided to distance myself."

"Unfortunately, it got easy to hold himself back from you, when you started wanting to spend more time with Granny and Mac." Mom pulled a tissue from her pocket and dabbed her eyes.

"Nick, when Kristy died..." Dad choked up and sniffed, hard. "When Kristy died, I wasn't there for you."

Nick finally lifted his eyes to his father. "No, you weren't." Seeing the devastation on his dad's face, he closed his eyes for a second and tempered his response. "It's okay, Dad."

"No, it's not. Look at me, Son." He stared straight into Nick's eyes, anger simmering. "It devastated me, and I didn't want to reach out to you for fear you'd see me crumble."

Seriously? This was the reason he'd been so cold during the hospitalization, funeral, and finding out his first grandchild had perished? Nick's anger threatened to explode within him. He could feel his blood pumping in his veins. "You didn't want to look weak?"

Dad shook his head. "Holdover from Grandpa. He told me a real man never lets 'em see you sweat. Or Cry. Or grieve openly." He chuckled grimly. "I knew, as I got older, that he was a hard man, but it was what kept me from letting Mac in, and it kept me from opening up to you and your mom."

"And it started because of a history of angry men in your family."

"No." His gaze went from Nick to Mom, a different demeanor on his face. "It started because I wasn't man enough to let God change my heart completely. I always kept a part of me for myself. It hasn't been easy, and God hasn't let me get away with it by any means." Dad cleared his throat. "I hope both of you can forgive me."

Nick felt anger tighten around his heart. Does Dad deserve forgiveness? He'd lied to him his whole life, and when he needed his father most, he distanced himself. Should he be forgiven?

No.

Not now.

Maybe someday. He stood up as his mother hugged his dad, and turned when he heard the crunch of gravel in the driveway. He felt the band around his chest loosen as he recognized Lisa's Explorer, and was thankful for the buffer.

Nick walked toward her vehicle, an expression on his face she'd only seen glimpses of before now. He was hurting, and he was angry.

She rubbed sweaty palms on her jeans and jumped out of her SUV. "Hey."

"Hey, yourself." He grinned, but the smile didn't meet his eyes. "What are you up to, out here on a Saturday?"

"I picked up some tile samples I wanted to drop off. Better than moving them twice. She glanced at Dan and Leticia. "You've got company.

"Mom and Dad came out to look at the house."

"Great. I figured they'd want to see it before we got too far along." She squinted a little in the sun and put her hand over her eyes, lowering her voice. "He didn't know the tunnels were there, did he?"

"So he said. Right now, I'm not sure what Dad knows and doesn't know." He glanced toward them and back to her, flexing his hands before stuffing them into the pockets of his jeans. "I'm learning things today that are brand-new facts for me."

Lisa didn't want to pry. It wasn't her business, but Nick needed to vent somewhere. If not to her, then to someone. "Are you okay? Do you want me to call Del? He can come out if you need him."

He shook his head and reached for her hand. "No, I'm glad you're here."

That was a plus.

"Come on over and say hi to Mom and Dad." He tightened his grip and tugged her along behind him.

The unexpected physical contact made her wonder if she'd be tongue-tied by the time they reached his parents. He held on to her as if his life depended on it.

"Lisa, it's so good to see you." Leticia reached out to hug her, which made her let go of Nick's hand.

"It's good to see you, too, Mrs. Woodward." Lisa turned her attention Nick's dad, who seemed distracted. "How are you, Mr. Woodward?"

He focused on her then, and smiled. "Good to see you, Lisa, and call us Dan and Leticia. So you're working on the old place? Lots of memories here and some of them include your dad."

She smiled, caught off guard by his sudden friendliness. She glanced up at Nick, whose face looked like it was carved in granite. *Ouch.*

"Dad told me about the two of you collaborating on FFA projects in high school."

Dan nodded. "Steve did the grunt work, and I made the presentations. We made a good team." Like Nick, Dan's smile was there, on the surface, but the way his eyes kept slipping toward Nick gave every indication of unfinished business.

"Dad said the same of you."

"Would you like to see the inside of the house? We're still in the rough phase, but you will see several changes already." Nick turned and started walking toward the house before anyone could say anything.

Lisa glanced at Leticia, hurting at the grief on her face as her husband walked past her and followed Nick.

"Are you okay?" Lisa touched her arm gently.

"I'll be fine. Men, right?" Tears collected on the older woman's lashes as she smiled.

With her own tears near the surface, for reasons she wasn't sure of, Lisa nodded and said, "Shall we?"

"Let's." Nick's mother slipped her arm through Lisa's and they walked to the refurbished front porch.

Nick was already showing his dad where they had taken out the wall, and Dan walked around, shaking his head. "Mama would have loved this, you know. Back when she was mistress of this house, you didn't think about these kinds of changes, or about what would make it more efficient."

Lisa chuckled. "I know. Kitchens were small and the dining rooms were big. This tells me houses were designed by men who thought women should be in the kitchen by themselves to prepare food for a huge family." She smiled at Dan, noticing the familiar hairline and brow so like Nick's.

"And yet Mama only had me. We rattled around in this big old house, but she loved it." He paused at the door to the basement and turned to speak to Nick. "Now I want to see what all the commotion has been about."

"You're sure you didn't know about the tunnels?" Nick asked his dad point-blank and Lisa's heart jumped a bit, feeling the tension in the air.

Dan sighed and closed his eyes for a moment. His face reddened and then went pale. When he responded, it was in measured phrases. "I knew there was an old cellar at the homeplace, but I had no idea there was a system of tunnels connecting our cellar to that one. I don't know if Mama knew or not. She never mentioned them to me, and Grandpa never told me. Maybe if he'd lived longer, he would have told me when I was older. He was good at keeping secrets."

Nick stared at his father as if trying to gauge whether or not he was telling him the truth. There must have been something that satisfied Nick because he nodded and went to the basement door. "Watch the first step. We haven't fixed it yet."

"It was always a little lower than it should be." Dad snorted when his foot hit the first step down. "But it's worse than it was."

Lisa laughed. "That's exactly what Nick said the first time we came down here."

"Well, I couldn't have you falling down the steps on me. One Reno with a broken leg is one too many." Nick glanced up at her standing at the top of the stairs, a grin on his face.

"Oh, that's right. How is Del? Nick told us about his fall." Leticia was picking her way down the stairs.

"He's doing well. Hoping to get the brace off and a smaller one on by next week. I hope he's better in time for plaster repair."

They reached the bottom of the steps. Thank goodness the smell was gone.

"So this is the door that used to be behind the cupboard." Dan shook his head and walked over to the door, now standing open. "I can't believe I never knew anything was down here."

"Do you think Granny knew anything about it?" Nick looked closely at his dad.

"No, because from the time I was big enough to carry two jars at a time, she kept me busy going up and down those steps fetching and carrying during canning season. I think if she had any idea anything was going on down here, she'd have kept me out of the basement." Dan smiled. "I guess she had your young legs to run her errands when you were here."

Nick emitted a short laugh. "You better believe it." He took a deep breath and turned his gaze to Lisa. "She canned enough for herself and half the county, seemed like."

"It's what women did back then." Leticia laughed and turned to Nick. "Remember when we cleaned out my parents' house after your grandma died? She always joked that our inheritance would be glass canning jars, and she wasn't kidding."

"I remember." He quirked a brow at his mom. "I don't remember bringing any of them home."

"I brought back some of the actual antique jars, but for decorative purposes only. The rest went for a good cause, so I don't feel a smidge of guilt."

Nick's mother, the peacemaker, winked at Lisa. She grinned back, observing the family dynamic. When she'd arrived, Nick was tense, angry, and searching for a way out. He had relaxed somewhat, although she could still see the tension in the set of his jaw when he was quiet.

Nick had his father's intensity, but his mother's calm exterior. Whether or not it was a good thing was still up for debate. What she couldn't figure out was Nick's need for her as a buffer between himself and his parents.

24

"What are you doing here on a Saturday?"

Nick had been quiet since his parents left a few minutes earlier. She felt the tug of his question. Why had she come over today? The tile samples could have stayed in her truck until Monday. There was nothing here that had to be done today, but something made her think she needed to make a few notes while the workmen weren't here. Or did she want to soak the house in while she could? Maybe she was meant to be here, at this moment.

She shrugged her shoulders and grinned. "Honestly?"

He snorted. "Are you in the habit of lying to me?"

"No." She felt the heat on her face. Why, oh why did she have to blush at the drop of a hat?

"Whatever brought you out here, I'm glad." He turned his gaze toward the big white house.

"Any reason in particular?" She turned to watch him as he stared straight ahead. At least he'd forgotten his question.

"Several." He was quiet again. After a few agonizing seconds, he turned toward her. "But mostly because I'm not sure what I would have said to my parents if you hadn't been here."

"I felt that vibe when I got here." Should she ask questions? Or wait until he was ready to share? She had no place in his life, other than as a friend. She wanted to ask all kinds of questions about his family, about why he seemed so aloof from his dad, about why his mother seemed to always be standing in the gap between them. It had to be exhausting for her.

"I wanted to punch Dad in the jaw and tell him where to go."

Her heart ramped up. "Do I dare ask why?"

"Dad has been a thorn in my side for a long time. There were times I may as well have not had a dad."

"I'm sorry." Tears threatened when she thought about her dad, stubborn as he was, and the loving relationship they had. She knew there were many kinds of relationships between fathers and their children, and it made her sad to think Nick had missed out on a loving relationship that would have taught him so much about relating to the world.

"Me, too." Nick shoved his hands in his pockets. "I think I was mad at him, at first, because he wouldn't come and visit Granny. She always seemed sad when Mom brought me to stay a few weeks in the summer. Dad always said he had to work, but it was awkward enough I knew something wasn't right."

"I can't imagine."

"I can't, either. Granny was a jewel. She and Granddad were happy together. She cooked, or worked in the garden most of the day, then sang and played the piano at night when I was there. Granddad taught me how to fish and basic carpentry work—he had been a carpenter in his younger days—and let me help him around the farm." He grinned at Lisa, then looked down. "The only time I saw her sadness was when I brought up Dad, and asked questions about when he was a boy. She tried to hide it, but I could tell it hurt her."

"Did you ever ask him about it?"

By now they were sitting together on the front steps, watching as the shadows began to lengthen. It was mid-summer, so the days were long, making the extended twilight a sweet relief from the heat of the day.

He shook his head. "No. I asked Mom, and she recommended I leave it be. She assured me Dad loved his mother and there were some things I didn't understand. I would understand when I grew up, she said."

He's grown-up now. Lisa stole a glance at him, seeing the same hard countenance he'd had on his face earlier. Yes, there had been words before she'd arrived. She turned her attention to her hands, clasped together on her knees.

"He told me Granddad wasn't his father."

She whipped her head around to scrutinize him, working hard to lift her jaw off the ground. "He's kept this a secret all your life?"

"All. My. Life."

Lisa tucked her hand through his arm at his elbow next to her and he put his other hand on top of hers. "Did he give you a reason why?" She tried to reconcile her curiosity with the feelings his touch stirred in her. She was having a hard time meeting his eyes. There was something in her that told her that even a glimpse into his eyes combined with his touch would get her into trouble. Fast.

He stroked her fingers absently. "Said he'd rather I thought he didn't get along with his dad than the truth that his father was an outlaw bootlegger with my grandfather."

"Whoa." She turned and caught him staring at her. After a few seconds he turned his face away from her, narrowing his eyes.

"When Kristy died, and the baby..." He cleared his throat and gazed, unfocused, on the countryside. "When they died, I couldn't figure out why Dad wasn't there for me. He was there, but not. It was as if he stayed above it all. Everyone else was grieving, and he was just, well, there."

"I'm so sorry." Tears stood in her lashes but she didn't dare wipe them away. She was afraid if she made a sudden movement, the moment would be over.

He squeezed her hand. "I know. He told me, today, how much it grieved him when Kristy died, and it made me so angry."

His emphasis on the last two words came with an uncomfortable squeeze that almost hurt. Almost.

"Maybe he has been afraid to be honest with you." She thought about her dad, and about his heart attack. Men tended to withhold information that might hurt someone, or make them feel uncomfortable.

He nodded. "I know, now. I think he thought if he let go of part of the truth, he'd have to let go of all of it."

"We're all like that to a certain extent."

He gave her a half grin. "No, I can't imagine you holding back."

"Oh, honey, you have no idea." She laughed abruptly and shook her head. The things she could tell him. She had made herself a pro at keeping things to herself, starting at a young age.

"You were pretty quiet when we first met, but I envied Del having a sister."

"Are you kidding me?" She turned with what she hoped was complete incredulity.

"I am not." He poked himself in the chest. "Only child here, remember? I don't even have many cousins. Jake is one of three."

"I never thought of that. My family has been around here for generations, and most of them are still here."

"Exactly. You have built-in friends and a brother who loves you." He pulled her up by the hand and stood in front of her, smiling. "Thank you."

"For what?" The golden hour of sunset shone on his face and it was all she could do to keep from reaching up to touch his cheek.

"For listening. Do you think Del would mind if I borrowed you from time to time since I don't have a sister?" He gave her a puzzled look, which almost made her laugh out loud.

Being Nick Woodward's sister was the last thing on her mind.

If they didn't get out of there soon, he would kiss her, and it would be the end of their friendship. On second thought, how badly did he need another friend?

Nick dropped her hand and, once again, stuffed his hands in his pockets. They'd be safe there.

"Not to change the subject, but did you have plans for this evening?" He didn't want to break it up yet. Somehow, he needed to be in her presence. He didn't want to think, but he needed to feel, for a change. And when he was with her, he felt plenty.

"Actually, I did have plans."

Great. Probably a date with the tall, blond, and handsome sheriff. "I'm sorry. I've kept you here and you have been itching to get away."

"Not really." She held up her hand, ticking off each activity one at a time. "Go over some music for tomorrow, take a long hot bath, give myself a pedicure, research reproduction light switches, and watch an old movie."

"Hoo. Hard to compete with that."

"Right?" She arched an eyebrow at him. "Did you have something in mind?"

"How does pizza sound?"

She nodded thoughtfully. "I could be persuaded."

"What's the movie?"

Lisa grinned. "It might be right up your alley, but I'm afraid of the ramifications."

"How come?"

"It's *Mr. Blandings Builds His Dream House.*"

"That's a new title for me."

"I'm sure it is. It was made in 1948, and stars Cary Grant and Myrna Loy." She laughed. "Yes, it's black and white, and it's about a city fellow and his wife who decide to move to the country and they buy a money pit."

He linked his fingers in hers again as he threw his head back and laughed out loud. "I promise not to give up on this old barn as long as you don't."

"There's one thing you've yet to learn about me." She poked him in the chest. "I never give up."

Nick was more than ready to test that theory.

25

⸙

"I hope he's not allergic to cats."

Lisa flew into the house and grabbed her duster. Cat hair, everywhere. Her stick vacuum in the tiny linen closet was charged and ready, and this was yet another time she was glad to have the equivalent of a tiny house.

She had made a quick stop at the office to pick up the journal while Nick drove into Marion for the pizza. As soon as she got home, she started water boiling on the stove to make sweet tea. Some of her married friends had received "iced tea makers" in their wedding showers, but she couldn't tell theirs was any better than hers, so she continued to make it the same way her mother and grandmothers did.

Dumping a cup of sugar into her gallon pitcher, she stirred up the hot liquid and then filled it the rest of the way with ice.

Surveying her public spaces in approval, she checked the clock and hurried into her bedroom to change into clean jeans and a shirt. Going through her drawer to pull out a tank top to wear under her button-up shirt, she saw the manila folder tucked carefully in the bottom.

She pulled it out and opened it, smiling at the sketch of Del and Nick she'd drawn on the quad at Murray State University. It was a simple pencil drawing, but it showed her acumen as an artist. Why didn't she spend more time drawing and painting? Because she was too busy being sensible.

Maybe she should show this to Nick. No. Not yet. She remembered she had started the drawing as a simple landscape of the trees and architecture of the campus, but they were sitting there, blocking her view of Lovett Auditorium, and she couldn't ask them to leave. It should be framed. Maybe even give it to Del for a keepsake. *Lord knows he needs more art on his walls.* She put the folder on top of the dresser to think about later.

Her clock told her she would only have about twenty minutes until Nick arrived with the pizza, so she switched out her sneakers for slip-on flats she could kick off while she watched television. Dessert. She should think about dessert.

Pulling a brush through her auburn curls, she stopped to focus on herself in the mirror. Usually, she took a cursory glance to make sure everything was in place, but her mind kept racing, thinking about Nick, about how it had felt when he took her hand earlier. Twice. It felt right. Good, even.

She wasn't interested in the position of a surrogate sister, best friend, or confidante. It had been months since she'd been on a date if you didn't count the fix-up at Mel and Jake's house. That didn't count. Did this?

Was Nick considering this a date? Or did he think of this as two buddies hanging out, eating pizza, and watching an old movie because they didn't have anything better to do? The idea that he might think of the evening like that almost made her angry.

Almost. Would she settle for a platonic friendship? Sometimes she thought "settle" was her middle name.

Hair brushed out, she pulled it up in a comfortable messy bun and slipped in the gold earrings she'd left on her bathroom vanity. Applying lip gloss, she turned her head this way and that to get a full picture, then put her hands on the vanity and stared into her own eyes. "Honey, you look good."

Nick pulled into Del's driveway on a whim. When they roomed together, they shared clothes constantly. Maybe he had a shirt he could change into. He'd gotten hot and sweaty at the house, and he still had about twenty minutes before the pizza would be ready.

The front door was open, the screen door latched on the inside, so he rang the doorbell.

"Just a minute." Del's voice came from the back of the house.

He called out. "It's Nick."

When Del hobbled to the door, he took the old-fashioned hook out of the eye and held it open for Nick to enter. "Hey. What are you doing in the neighborhood?"

Suddenly he felt very awkward. How would Del feel about the idea of him spending time with his sister?

Nick took a deep breath. "I need a favor, and if you don't want to do it, I won't be upset. In fact, if you don't want me involved, I'll be fine."

Del tilted his head and narrowed his eyes at his friend. He didn't say anything for a few seconds, but it felt like several minutes to Nick.

"Was that cryptic enough for you?"

Del laughed out loud. "Yeah, cryptic was the word I was looking for, and couldn't quite put my finger on it." He shook his head. "I don't have a clue what you're talking about, but you know you can ask anything. Can you sit for a minute?"

"Thanks." Nick perched on the sofa close to Del's recliner and wove his fingers together between his knees.

"What's the favor?"

"Before I ask the favor, I need to ask your opinion."

"Since when do you need my opinion?"

The words seemed to come out of a place he had pushed down for the last two years. He didn't deserve it, but it was coming out. "Since I may want to date your sister." Nick tried to avoid eye contact but finally had to raise his head to look into the smiling face of his best friend. "I take it you're not against the idea?"

"I have two things to say about you dating Lisa." Del leaned forward. "First, it's about time."

"Our timing hasn't been the best."

"No kidding. She had a crush on you all the way back to college, and if you tell her I told you, I'll deny it."

"Understood." He looked up at his friend. "Back up. Seriously? She had a crush on me?" He could tell Lisa didn't dislike him, but she'd kept her feelings well-hidden.

"Oh yeah."

"Why didn't you try to fix us up?"

Del shrugged. "Because Lisa wasn't ready, and I was immature enough to think it might not be a good idea for my best friend to get involved with my sister."

"I understand." Nick thought for a few minutes about what might have been if he and Lisa had been together from the start. He had loved Kristy. Deeply. And if he'd fallen for Lisa then, he'd have never known the great love, and great loss, he'd had with his wife.

And would that have been a bad thing? Did he deserve two loves in his life?

"What's the second thing?"

Del focused on him. "Don't be stupid."

Nick squinted one eye in confusion. "I try not to be. In what context, if you don't mind."

Del was serious, now. "Don't break her heart."

The last thing he wanted was a broken heart, for Lisa or himself. "I don't plan to."

"Yeah, yeah, yeah...I know all about 'plans.'"

He sat there for a few moments. He'd only seen Del this serious a few times. His laid-back persona and shaggy haircut made everyone think he was an easy-going guy who leaned on everyone else, but he knew that wasn't the real story. When it came to work, faith, or family, Del was sharp as a tack.

"Hey, what was the favor you needed?"

Nick chuckled. "Do you have a clean shirt I could borrow?"

26

Lisa looked at the clock for the tenth time and frowned. What was taking so long? Maybe there was a run at the pizza place and they were behind. Or maybe he'd changed his mind and decided to skip out while he was closer to home. No. He wouldn't do that without letting her know.

She had the DVD in the player, brownies in the oven, and ice in the glasses. She's spent the last fifteen minutes carefully turning the pages of the journal kept by his great-grandmother. Surely he would be there soon. It was just now dark.

About the time she considered dumping the ice melting in their glasses, she saw vehicle lights glint through her living room windows.

The timer on the oven checked, she did a quick inspection of herself in the mirror next to the front door. Decorative? Yes. Useful? Oh, yes.

She glanced through the sidelight as he rang the doorbell. Taken aback, she opened the door to see him carrying a pizza and a bouquet of flowers.

"I would have bought a drink, but I wasn't sure what you'd prefer."

"Flowers?" She took them and immediately pulled them to her face to smell them. "They're beautiful. Where did you find them this time of the evening?"

He reddened a bit. "At the grocery store."

She smiled. "Life in a small town, eh?"

"Yes."

"And you changed shirts." She looked him in the eye. "Surely you didn't go all the way home?"

"No, I didn't."

"So...?"

"I borrowed a shirt from Del."

At that, she burst out laughing.

"Hey, you changed, too, if I'm remembering correctly." Nick raised an eyebrow."

"Busted." She led him to the kitchen, where she pulled out a vase for her flowers. "I remember you and Del sharing clothes in college. I was always glad you didn't have the same color hair, or I might have whacked you on the back of the head sometime when you were wearing Del's duds."

"I probably needed it." He was looking at her strangely. What was he thinking?

Tilting her head, she paused, wondering. "I never thought so."

"I find that hard to believe." Nick snorted quietly.

Hmmm. How to respond? She had a sudden impulse, which was strange since she wasn't known for her impulsivity. She paused in filling the glasses and held up a finger. "Wait here. I want to show you something."

Picking up the folder from the top of the dresser, she caught a glimpse of herself in the mirror and stopped. Her eyes were huge. And scared. What if he didn't like it? What if he took it wrong? What if...

She shook her head furiously and muttered to herself. "I'm tired of saying 'what if.'"

Nick looked up when she came back into the kitchen, carrying the folder. "Are you okay?"

Smiling, she handed him the folder. "I'm fine. I found this earlier and thought you might want to see it."

When he opened the folder, his eyebrows went up in surprise. "This is amazing." He shook his head. "Why are you not creating art for a living?"

For some reason, his question surprised her. While she had enjoyed her art classes attached to her design major, she had never felt confident enough in her talent to go beyond her classmates seeing her art.

Tears rushed to her eyes even while she smiled. "I never thought I was any better than anybody else, I guess." It wasn't the practical thing to do. Being an artist wasn't for a girl who was sensible.

He continued staring at the piece, smiling and shaking his head. "You were sitting on the grass, close to this bench, weren't you?"

"I was. I was trying to draw Lovett Auditorium and the spring blooming trees, but you and Del plopped down there in my sight-line."

"You should have told us to get lost." He laughed.

Shrugging her shoulders, she laughed with him. "I decided to make the best of the situation and practice on my people-drawing skills."

"I think you'd already perfected them." He looked at her curiously. "Do you paint, too?"

Lisa bit her lip and nodded. "A little. I haven't in a long time, but it's relaxing." She glanced at the landscape over her fireplace, and his eyes followed hers.

"That one?"

She nodded. "I painted it right after college before I moved to Texas."

He walked over to it, pizza forgotten for a few minutes. "I'm speechless."

"Just what I want to hear from a movie date." Did she say that out loud? She laughed and broke the spell. Maybe he would forget about her art. After all, she almost had.

Nick was glad they were watching a movie. It gave him time to think. He enjoyed the antics of Cary Grant and Myrna Loy, but more than anything he found pleasure in watching Lisa. She liked living through the eyes of the characters. Was it easier than life through her own eyes?

The drawing, the painting. They were incredible. After learning from Del of her crush during their college days, he saw the drawing in a different light. Her touch was careful. Sure. Loving. It ate at him, a little, that he'd taken her for granted back then.

But maybe Del was right. She wasn't ready, and at that point, it might have been a mistake. If they'd parted then, he'd never have known this adult version of Lisa. Would he rather have not had the years with Kristy? No. He could never regret it. He had been blessed. He'd always been taught, "The Lord giveth, and the Lord taketh away."

He'd railed against it, but it didn't do any good. Kristy was gone, and it was up to him to get on with what was left of his life. He looked down at his left hand. He had recently stopped wearing his wedding ring for what he told himself were safety reasons on the job, but there was still a tan line where he'd had it on most of the time for the last six years. Maybe it was time he left it off for good.

"Brownies?" Lisa had paused the DVD and turned toward him, smiling.

"No one can accuse me of foregoing brownies."

"I also have ice cream." She lifted a brow enticingly, having no idea his mind was going everywhere but the freezer when she did that.

"You do know the way to a man's heart, don't you?"

When she laughed, he felt it to his toes. She got up and crossed in front of him to go to the kitchen, and stood to follow her.

"You didn't have to get up." She flitted around the kitchen, secure in her own space.

"I needed to stretch my legs anyway." He glanced at her small dining table. "I see you brought the journal."

"Do you mind? I thought maybe we could look through it while you're here."

"I'm glad you did." He leafed through the pages, noting, as she had, where the handwriting stopped. "I looked at the family tree in my grandmother's family Bible, and it shows Salina died in 1933."

Lisa looked up from cutting the brownies. "Whoa."

"Yeah. So my grandfather grew up without his mother, and Dad grew up without his father." What a family legacy.

"That could explain a few things."

"About?"

"About your dad." She licked her finger where she'd cleaned the gooey chocolate off the knife. "His anger."

Nick nodded. It explained more than he'd prefer to admit.

"Would you like coffee?" She pointed to the coffee maker on the corner of her countertop. "I've got beans already ground and it will just take a minute."

"Sure." He had a feeling he'd be up a while anyway. Closing the small book, he took a deep breath. "Let's not think about angry ancestors."

"Sounds good to me. Does coffee keep you awake?"

Nick chuckled. "I haven't slept well in so long, I have no idea. But it doesn't seem to matter."

"Coffee has never made me unable to sleep. In fact, sometimes it relaxes me to the point I sleep better." She measured out the ground coffee into the basket and turned it on. "I'll wait on dipping the ice cream until the coffee is done." Leaning a hip on the counter, she crossed her arms. "Is the movie giving you any ideas for the house?"

"I may have to rethink my color schemes." He raised his voice to quote Myrna Loy's character 'I want it to be a soft green, not as blue-green as a robin's egg, but not as yellow-green as daffodil buds.'"

"I love that part." Lisa shook with laughter. "But she was so poised." She sighed. "I'll bet she never fell through a porch."

"Maybe not, but she probably didn't have nearly as much fun as we have."

"She was married to Cary Grant." She gave him that "look" again.

"Myrna Loy?"

"No, silly, Mrs. Blandings. He's so sigh-worthy."

"What in the world is 'sigh-worthy'?" Laughter was starting to bubble up within him as the coffee began to make the sounds of finishing its process and Lisa reached toward the mug rack to retrieve a couple of cups.

She handed him a cup of steaming coffee and turned to dip the ice cream to go along with the warm brownies. "I suppose it's a really girlish phrase, isn't it?"

"Very. When I think of something being worthy of a sigh, I think of a finished house or a freshly-mowed lawn."

"Oh my." She put away the ice cream and gestured for them to return to the living area. She took her seat and explained after her first bite of brownie-and-ice cream. "Sigh-worthy is the description readers of romance give to the hero of the tale. The love interest." Her cheeks reddened when she glanced at him. "If the hero doesn't make you sigh, then there's something wrong with the romance."

"So you consider Cary Grant sigh-worthy? Isn't he awfully old for a girl your age?"

"Well, yeah, and he's dead, so there's that."

Nick put his coffee and dessert plate on the table in front of him and laughed out loud. "Who else?"

"As in, modern day?" She pondered a moment, tapping her finger on her chin.

He'd seen her do it before, and it intrigued him.

"Captain America and Daniel Craig."

"You mean Chris Evans as Captain America?"

"Yes and no. The character is what makes him so sigh-worthy, to me."

"And Daniel Craig?"

She turned to look him in the eye. "Having been raised on every 007 since Sean Connery, and taught to disregard all but the original, I believe Daniel Craig the best Bond since."

She was serious. And she'd given this a lot of thought, apparently. What was it about a girl who loved the idea of a man not only being a protector, but also a champion? The James Bond character wasn't known for his integrity in his personal relationships, but like Captain America, he would go to great lengths to protect and defend those he loved or to whom he was loyal.

"It's a lot to live up to." He spoke quietly, staring into her eyes.

When her lips relaxed into a smile, his gaze slipped to her lips and she involuntarily caught her bottom lip between her teeth. Self-conscious. Uncertain.

When her eyes dropped to his lips, he knew he was a goner.

27

"What's up with you, girlfriend?"

Mel got Lisa's attention when she elbowed her in the ribs as they sat in their Bible study class waiting for it to start. There was chattering all around them, and Lisa sat there, staring straight ahead, her mind anywhere but in the classroom.

A study of the book of Lamentations wasn't what she was thinking about. Maybe 1 Corinthians, chapter thirteen? The love chapter.

"Sorry. I stayed up too late watching a movie last night." She gave Mel a sidelong glance, not ready to talk to anyone about Nick. The kiss they had shared was too tender. Too new.

"Um-hmm." She narrowed her eyes at her friend. "You have a secret."

"What...?" Sometimes being an open book was aggravating.

As she opened her mouth, a shadow fell over them, and there stood Clay. "Good morning, ladies. Is that seat taken?" He was indicating the seat on the other side of Lisa. Unfortunately for her, fortunately for the teacher, the class was filling up this morning.

Melanie narrowed her eyes at Lisa and then nodded approval. "Hi Clay. I'm saving this one for Jake, but that one is free. Isn't it?" Her pointed gaze landed squarely on Lisa.

"It's a free classroom, Clay." She shifted her legs over so he could get himself past her. "If I didn't have to slip out early, we would slide down, but then I'd be climbing over you."

He grinned at her as he folded himself into the metal chair. "That would have been fine, too."

She gave him a small smile and turned back to Mel, speaking softly. "Where were we?"

"You haven't been able to keep a secret from me since third grade." Then Mel did it. She rolled her eyes, lowering her voice as Lisa had.

"Sometimes a girl—"

"Honey, I hate to be the one to tell you, but you're not a girl anymore. You are a grown-up woman." Now she was elevating the eyebrow. Even at the puffy stage of pregnancy, as in, about to pop, Melanie's brows and makeup were impeccable. The arch of her brow was perfect, and she was using her "I'm pregnant, I'm tired, and I'm not giving grace to anybody or anything" voice.

"All right, sometimes a woman wants to think things through before spilling her guts like a seventh-grader on the playground."

There. That should shut her up. But, by the expression on her face, Lisa knew it was a fleeting dream.

"Sounds like we need to have a girls' day."

Saved by the bell. She was so glad to see the teacher, Gary, take the podium in front of the class of twenty-somethings and thirty-somethings. He opened his mouth to start when the door in the back of the classroom opened and he called out, "Welcome. I'm sure someone will scoot over and make room."

Lisa glanced back and straight into the eyes of Nick Woodward, where they held. The left side of his lips quirked up, and then he checked the seat next to her. *Great.* It would be Clay sitting there. Melanie and Jake were signaling to her that they could scoot down another seat to let Nick sit on the end. Lisa got the message to Clay, who shifted to the next seat, but Jake stayed in his seat and held on to Melanie, probably in case they had to leave in a hurry, and Lisa ended up sitting between Clay and Nick.

After the previous evening, the last thing she wanted was to feel awkward, but she supposed she would feel awkward until the day she died.

⁓

It hadn't been Nick's plan to show up at church in Clementville in time for Sunday school, but when he woke up at five AM unable to get back to sleep, he'd cleaned up and gotten in his truck. He started driving and thinking, and the thinking led to praying. The praying led to more thinking about Lisa and the tenderness of her lips the night before. Those thoughts made him know he didn't want to go another day without seeing her, and he knew where she would be.

Where he didn't expect her to be was seated next to Clay Lacey. To be fair, the room was full, and they were old friends. She was also sitting with his cousin's wife. Not knowing who had arrived first, he couldn't jump to conclusions.

When he settled into the seat between Melanie and Lisa, he whispered to her. "Are you busy after church?"

She blushed adorably and shook her head. What would she do if he took her hand? What would Clay do?

"No." Her eyes cut between him and the teacher.

Good. If Clay hadn't been sitting on the other side of Lisa, he might have waited to ask her after church, but as it was, he wanted to get 'dibs' for the afternoon. "We'll talk later."

"I have to leave class early. Are you staying for the service?"

Nodding, he smiled. "Are you playing?" Of course, she was. "I wouldn't miss it." He listened to the teacher for a few moments, then whispered toward her, his eyes never leaving the front of the classroom. "Don't make any plans." He cut his eyes toward her for an answer.

Mouthing "okay," she grinned at him and opened her Bible,

182

offering to share when she saw he didn't have one with him. Under cover of her Bible, their hands touched, and Nick encircled her pinky with his. It delighted him to see her tug at her bottom lip again, but it certainly didn't help him to concentrate on what the Bible-study teacher was saying.

"When will Steve and Roxy be home? It seems like they've been gone long enough." Pastor Aaron shook her hand as he made his way back to the altar area after the service was over.

"Next week." She was gathering up her music, Bible, and purse, placing all her items in one big bag. "They're on the train for a few days. It goes through Montana, North Dakota, Minnesota, then down to Chicago and St. Louis."

"If anybody deserves an extended honeymoon, those two do."

"I know. I'm glad to see them take a trip like this. It's a once-in-a-lifetime vacation."

"Maybe someday I can take my wife on an extended trip." He scanned the auditorium. "But in the meantime, I'd better rescue her from our children. See you this afternoon?"

"I'll be here." Always. She hadn't missed many rehearsals or services in her lifetime. Maybe someday she would have a honeymoon trip. She sighed and picked up her bag, making her way to the exit, where Nick was waiting.

"Let me carry your bag." Nick took it from her hand and walked with her toward the parking lot. "That was a big sigh."

"It had nothing to do with what I said about men who are sigh-worthy, if that's what you're thinking." She grinned and took the bag from him as they got to her car.

"Sorry to hear that." Nick glanced around. Her car was the last one left in the lot behind the church, and his truck was in the next lot over.

She'd been there since seven thirty in the morning for sound check, and there wasn't much competition for spots at that time.

"I wondered if you'd like to go on a picnic." She thought he was going to put his hands in his pockets, but then changed his mind and took her hand. She liked it. Her hand felt right there.

The sky was clear and blue, and the humidity was down for a day in late July. "Sounds like fun. Where did you have in mind?"

"Cave-in-Rock?" His smile had grown when she acquiesced.

It made her feel a little bit powerful, the ability to broaden his smile.

"Perfect. A ferry ride and a picnic. What girl could refuse?"

"I was hoping you'd say that." He looked down at their entwined hands. "We need to talk."

"I know."

"I was hoping I didn't overstep last night."

She felt heat rush to her face as she, too, looked down, mesmerized by his thumb gently rubbing her hand. For the first time, she noticed the white line around his left ring finger. After her initial sighting of his wedding ring, she had tried not to pay attention to his hands, but now she came to the realization that he seemed to be making a serious effort to get on with life.

She peeked up at him and saw the serious expression on his face. "You didn't."

He nodded. Was he choked up? What was he thinking right now? How did one go from being happily married, expecting a baby, to being all alone again? How did you go on from such grief and find yourself drawn to someone else? Was this real, or was she just the best option? She couldn't ask those questions. Not now, anyway. But they would be there, in the back of her mind, until they were answered, one way or another.

"Follow me home and I'll change into my picnic duds."

The smile on his face relaxed his features. "I brought extra clothes, too."

"Oh, I thought maybe you'd need to swing by Del's house and borrow some more clothes." She laughed. The serious mood was broken, for now, and she was glad. She was tired of thinking. She wanted to feel.

Nick watched as Lisa expertly navigated the parking lot entry known for flattening exhaust pipes. She could certainly handle large vehicles and broken houses.

Could she handle a broken man?

His phone buzzed, and he looked at it. Del. With a half grin, he hit the Accept button.

"Hey, Del. What's up?"

"I had parking lot security at church, so I didn't get a chance to see you. You got any plans this afternoon?"

Nick observed the beautiful day as he strolled across the lot toward his truck. "I do. Going on a picnic with your sister."

"Ah."

The line went quiet. Had the call been dropped?

"Del?"

"Yeah, I'm here."

He could hear him coughing. "Are you okay?"

He wasn't coughing. He was laughing.

"Nick, I'm practically perfect. Glad to hear you're not sitting on your hands."

"Yeah, well..."

"Listen, she can get bossy if you're not careful."

"I've seen a little bit of that side of her." It wasn't the side he was thinking about right now, but he'd keep that to himself.

"I'm sure you have." Del paused. "Since Dad isn't here, do we need to have the 'she's my baby sister and you'd better not break her heart' speech?"

"I think you already gave me that."

"Oh yeah. When I told you not to be stupid." Del's mellow laugh made Nick shake his head.

"That's the one." How had he let his relationship with Del go to the back burner for so long?

"We haven't had the 'what are your intentions' talk, though." Del snorted. "Maybe it's the one I should have with Lisa."

"Don't you dare." A stolen kiss and holding her hand weren't cause for such. Yet.

"I won't." When Nick didn't say anything, Del chuckled. "Lighten up, man."

"Sorry." He took a deep breath as he reached for the door handle of his truck. "I haven't...well...since..."

"Are you telling me you haven't dated since Kristy?" Del drew in a breath. "That's tough. Listen, you need anything, you let me know." He waited a few seconds. "I mean it, Nick. Clean shirt, a listening ear, info about my sister. Name it, and it's there."

He had the blessing of her brother. Del always liked to go with the flow, while he tended to weigh his options. Maybe it was time to take a page from Del's playbook and see where this led.

"Thanks, Del. I appreciate it. I don't want to rush into anything, but I don't want to miss an opportunity, either." He paused, wondering if he dared ask his next question. If he didn't, he'd wonder all day. "I do have one question."

"What's that?"

"Is there anything going on between Lisa and Clay?"

Lisa's head went up at the sound of a light rap on the door. He was here. She glanced at herself in the mirror, pleased she had taken pains with her makeup before she left for church early that morning. Her color was high, and she felt a flutter as she opened her screen door. "Hey."

"Hey, yourself." He came in and leaned on the doorjamb, hands in his pockets, smiling at her.

Cocking her head to one side, she narrowed her eyes at him. "What's up?"

"Nothing. Just thinking."

"About?"

"I just got off the phone with Del."

"Oh yeah, he was working parking lot today, wasn't he?" Lisa walked into the kitchen and pulled out cold cuts, cheese, and bread. "I thought we could make sandwiches to take for our picnic. Barbecued ham and cheese okay?"

"Sounds good. I brought cookies from Our Daily Bread." He lifted his eyebrows.

"Yum. I love their cookies. We can save the brownies for later." She glanced up at him. Was she expecting too much? What did she mean by "we"?

"Del said something about you having to be back by five?"

"I have band rehearsal, then church. Is that okay?" She lowered her brows. "If you don't think we'll have time, we can eat here, or over at your place."

"I think we'll be fine." He watched as she put the sandwiches, chips, and a few bottles of water in a basket. "Is it okay if I go back to church tonight?"

She raised startled eyes to him. "Of course it is." She grabbed the quilt she had laid out for the picnic. You never knew if there would be picnic tables available on a Sunday afternoon. "Evening service doesn't start until six, but you can hang out while we're in rehearsal if you want."

"I thought I'd drive around my place and get there by six if that's okay."

"You should call Del. He might want to hang out."

Nodding, he took the basket from her. "I might. Ready?"

"Ready. Your truck or mine?"

He grinned at her. "Mine. It's where the cookies are."

"That settles that." She locked her front door and pushed the screen door shut, then turned to find Nick still on the porch.

"Thank you."

"For what?" She felt a shiver go up her spine, but in a good way. When he leaned down to kiss her softly on her upturned lips, she smiled into the kiss.

"For that."

Staring up into his dark eyes, she wondered for the millionth time if she was doing the right thing to get involved with Nick Woodward. A good man, yes. But the things he'd been through. How could her tiny, insignificant life compete? How could she? And did she want to?

28

About the time they cleaned up their picnic site, Nick heard a rumble of thunder. He pulled out his phone to check the weather app. "We may have to go to the cave another time. There's a storm brewing."

Lisa shaded her eyes to survey the intermittent clouds. "Is it me, or does the sky look a little strange?"

Sure enough, there was a green tinge to the sky abnormal for July in Kentucky–or anywhere else for that matter. "We'd better get back to the ferry if we want to get home before it hits."

Lisa was checking the weather app on her phone. When her eyes met his, he stopped what he was doing. "We're in a Tornado Watch, but Livingston County is in a warning, and they're just down the river from here."

"Let's go." He picked up the basket and Lisa gathered up the quilt, and they ran to the truck as rain began to fall. "I hope they don't close the ferry down."

"Maybe we can get on the last trip before the warning gets here."

The wind picked up, turning the leaves on the trees inside-out as the storm drew nearer.

The ferry captain was securing his slicker as he came over to the window. He kept glancing at the sky and the river, then at Nick and Lisa. "We're going to get across as quick as we can. You folks okay with that?"

"Yes, sir, we are. We live close to the other side, in Clementville."

"Good. Looks like a doozy coming upriver."

Nick began rolling up his window, then a thought stopped him. He called out to the captain. "Do you have a place to go out of the storm?"

The suntanned captain smiled, his teeth even whiter against his brown face. "We do. An Amish family on the next hill up told us to come to their place any time there's a storm and we get caught on the Kentucky side. Thanks for asking."

"No problem. Stay safe."

Nick rolled his window up and glanced over at his slightly-damp date. "You okay?"

"I'm fine. Not crazy about crossing in a storm, but I've done it before." She shrugged her shoulders and wrapped her arms around herself.

"Cold?" He reached behind him to get the quilt they'd snatched from the ground earlier. "Here. It's a little damp, but it might help." He tucked it around her gently, thinking seriously about kissing her but deciding against taking advantage of the situation. Time enough for that. He needed to keep his head, and the more he was with Lisa, the less critical thinking he seemed to be able to do.

"Thank you."

"You're welcome." He tore his eyes away from hers and leaned forward to look at the sky out the windshield.

The ride across was choppy, whitecaps on the river. At one point, the water was so rough that waves splashed up on the windshield, but the weather had caused the barges that would usually have the right-of-way to be safely moored, giving them a straight shot from Illinois to Kentucky.

When they got off the ferry onto Highway 91, both their cell phones began to blow up with weather emergency signals.

Nick peered at the sky through the windshield. "We need to get to my house. It's closer."

"Fine with me. Those clouds look positively apocalyptic." She shivered, even under the quilt.

The wording sounded like Del. Brother and sister might be more alike than he thought. "When we get there, bring the quilt. We may need it." He drove as fast as he dared, cutting the usual ten-minute drive to a fast five.

"At least your basement doesn't smell anymore."

"I guess we should be thankful for small mercies." He grimaced at the rain slashing the windshield as he stopped as close to the back door of the house as he could and pulled his key out to be ready. "We're going to have to make a run for it."

She nodded. "Don't worry about me. I'll be right behind you."

"Be careful."

"I will."

Nick took a deep breath and opened his door, then slammed it and ran to the back porch. He unlocked the door and looked back to see Lisa right behind him. Thank goodness.

"I don't think this will do us much good." Lisa held up the quilt that dripped from the hem. "It's a shame we don't have a dryer installed yet."

He took it from her and threw it over a ladder in the mudroom. He could hear what sounded like a freight train, but there were no train tracks left in the county.

A tornado was coming.

"Let's get downstairs." He paused and looked toward the kitchen. "Hang on. I'll get the flashlights, just in case."

<hr />

Lisa skipped down the stairs, then turned on lights as she came to the bottom. It had been so dry, it would take a while for the rainwater to make its way into the basement. Thunder boomed outside, and even underneath the house, she could feel the wind shift and become more violent.

"I hope the ferry guys got to safety. It sounds bad out there." Nick handed her a box and sat on the bottom step.

"You thought to get the cookies?" The longer she knew Nick Woodward, the more she loved him. *Wait. Do I love him?*

"Are you okay?"

He must have noticed her eyes when the fleeting thought went through her head because she knew her eyes must have gone totally round. "I-I'm fine." Her laugh was shakier than usual.

"Are you afraid of storms?" His concern touched her. Frankly, she was nervous.

She sat next to him and surveyed their stash for a cookie with lots of chocolate chips. "A little. A tornado came through south of Marion when I was in preschool, and our teachers herded us into the hallway for a 'tornado drill.'" She took a bite, then startled at a particularly loud clap of thunder. "We didn't know anything had happened. I remember Mom being pale and shaky when she arrived to pick me up, and I was so excited to tell her about the drill and how the teacher said we did everything exactly right."

"I remember that one. I was at school in Elizabethtown. We had a warning, but it went north of us."

Lisa rubbed her damp arms again, chilling at the thought of another tornado like the one she remembered. "Mom told me later she had been stopped on the highway while it was going on. She was about a quarter mile outside of the Crayne community when it hit, and then had to drive through the devastation after it was over. We drove out there the next day, with Dad, and it didn't hit me until I saw a house where a friend lived, completely demolished. I heard her tell Dad she cried all the way through Crayne that day, worried about me at preschool. I didn't understand it then, but I do now."

Nick nodded. "I always wanted to live on the beach, and Granny would say, 'But what about those hurricanes?'" He laughed. "I told her I'd rather know a hurricane was coming a week ahead than have a tornado bear down on me and the weather warnings not get to me in time."

"Exactly." She looked up the steps as the wind howled outside. "Is it just me, or did the lights go dim?"

"If your sight's going, mine is, too." He pushed the weather channel app on his phone, but there was no signal. "Nothing."

"I hope Del's able to get to his basement." Her eyes met Nick's, and he looked down at the goosebumps on her arms.

"Still cold?"

"Nervous, mainly, but it is a little chilly down here."

He put his arm around her and pulled her close. "Maybe that will help."

She felt warmer, all right. Much warmer.

She was worried. To be honest, so was he.

Nick tried to concentrate his attention on Lisa, and not on the sounds coming from above their heads. This house had been here for over a hundred years. Would it survive this storm?

He relished the feeling of Lisa in the crook of his arm. She had gone quiet after he'd pulled her closer. Did she regret coming out with him? The kiss they'd shared?

Did he regret it?

Part of him did. It was the part that had made a vow to love, honor, and cherish Kristy. But the vow was "'til death do us part," wasn't it? Kristy was gone. She wasn't coming back. How many times had he told himself this fact?

When the basement door flew open, he and Lisa jumped from the step. "Go through the door."

"To the tunnel?" She looked startled.

"We know the house won't fall in on us in there."

"But we don't know how stable the tunnel is."

"It's been there for a hundred years. I think it'll be okay for the next ten minutes." He grabbed her arm and pulled her toward the ancient door as debris showered down the stairwell.

Once inside, Nick turned on the flashlight and set it down on its end, illuminating the room. They shifted to sit on the floor against the door, and he pulled her close. "We'll be okay."

Her head fit the crook between his neck and shoulder perfectly. He heard her sniff and tilted her chin up so he could see her eyes. She was crying. "Really. We'll be fine."

"I know."

He glanced down at her lips. Mistake. Once he'd tasted them, he needed more, and he'd only captured them once today. Would kissing her now be a good distraction for her, or would it be taking advantage of the situation?

When her eyes met his, then shifted down to his lips, he was fairly certain she would welcome the distraction.

He had loved Kristy. Completely. He had wanted to build a life with her. He had planned to grow old with her.

Wanting Lisa felt both right and wrong at the same time. The part that felt right was validated when his lips met hers and she relaxed into his arms. Her kisses and the roaring of the turbulence above them combined to wipe away anything that had happened before. When the sounds of destruction above stopped, it got his attention.

He ended the kiss and looked down at Lisa. "It's over."

It's over? What's over? She didn't want his kiss to be over, because she felt that if he stopped kissing her, she would fly apart from sheer energy. She felt bereft when he stopped.

He disentangled himself to stand, then took her hand and pulled her up, not meeting her eyes.

Lisa got up to follow him, stopping short when he couldn't get the door to swing out. "Nick?" She was confused, and not only about the door not opening.

"I think it's stuck."

"Want me to lean on it, too?"

He considered her slight frame and smiled. "Let me try it again, then maybe I'll call in the big guns."

"Funny. Haha."

It was a relief to hear him chuckle.

He rattled the doorknob, and it turned easily. But no matter how hard he pushed, the door would not open. "There must be something wedged against it."

"Can we...?" She shook her head. "Nope. I started to say we could take it off at the hinges, but they're on the other side."

"And, we don't seem to have a hammer and screwdriver on us."

"They're on the other side of the door, unfortunately." A sudden thought made her stare at him. "Do you think the house is gone?"

"I think we'd have heard more noise if it had been demolished." He shoved against the door with his shoulder, wincing.

"Careful. All we need is for one of us to get hurt." She tested the door herself. "It moves slightly, but then it doesn't."

She checked her phone. Still no signal. "It's for sure we can't call anyone for help. Do you have any signal?"

"Nothing. I guess we can take our chances and head to the other end of the tunnel and walk back to the truck."

"No one knows where we are."

"Del knows we were going on a picnic, but not where."

"He won't think about us being here." She looked around at the relatively dry room, shivering at the thought of going back through the tunnel where they'd found the original corpse. "One question."

"What?" He eyed curiously.

"Is the trap door locked at the other end of the tunnel?"

In a different situation, she might have laughed when she saw his jaw sag. He raked his hand over his face and took a deep breath. "Of course it is. I put a new padlock on it last week."

29

Of all the stupid, ignorant...

"Nick."

She'd called his name twice, and now she took his hand to get his attention. His vision began to clear and he looked down at her in the dim light.

"Sorry."

"There's nothing to be sorry for." She squeezed his hand until she had his full attention. "We need to figure out how we're going to get out of here."

He nodded. She was right. Berating himself wasn't going to get them out of this literal hole in the ground. Once more. He'd try opening this door one more time, then he'd try something else. "Step back a minute."

As she did, he shoved at it with his shoulder. It gave ever so slightly, and then nothing.

"You're going to hurt yourself."

"Too late." His shoulder would be black and blue tomorrow.

"Anything we could use as a wedge?"

Head shaking, he was grim. "The door has to open out, and if there is something up against it..."

"I know." She looked around as if waiting for inspiration to strike. Getting her phone out, she shook her head. "Still no signal, and I'm almost out of juice."

"If it gets too low, use the wind-up flashlight. It has a phone charger built-in."

"Cool." Her eyebrow lifted in approval.

"Yeah, well, it won't open doors or pick locks for us, and we don't have a signal, so it's not as if we can use it to call anybody. If the tunnel goes closer to the surface, we may get a weak signal."

"We'll have to exit through the smaller tunnel that comes out on the bluff."

He stilled. "Where they found the skeleton. I never got to read the full report of the FBI investigation."

"Clay didn't give you a copy?" Lisa was incredulous.

"I'm not his favorite person right now." Nor would he ever be as long as no one had laid claim to Lisa's affections.

"That's ridiculous."

"I think he wanted to wait until they had ID'd the remains. And now Dad wants me to have the DNA testing done to see if it might be his father. My grandfather." He wouldn't get off on a tangent. "Okay then, let's try it."

"Do you think the river bluff tunnel is how they got in and out?"

He twisted his lips in a grim smile. "Probably at least an alternate entrance if they couldn't get to the trap door. Gotta have some way to get the contraband in circulation."

"You've got to let it go, Nick."

"Easier said than done." He gave her the light-weight wind-up flashlight and picked up the Maglite. "I'll go first in case we run across any hooligans or wild animals."

Lisa followed Nick closely. The flashlights illuminated the tunnel, but the occasional root threatened to trip them up or whack them in the face. It was obvious no one had used parts of it in years. "Do you think whoever killed the guy we found got in this way?" She was talking to his back, but he kept walking.

"Maybe." He stopped abruptly. "Hold up. There's another root hanging down." He took out his pocketknife and cut it out of the way.

They entered the larger room where they had found the desk and the journal earlier. "I wish we'd had more time to look over the journal." She heard scurrying in a corner and quickly shone her light in that direction.

"Me, too. It might shed light on a lot of things."

"When we get back home..."

"Provided home is still there. That was a bad storm."

"I know." She had dismissed all thoughts of what was going on aboveground. Being with Nick was enough. She hadn't thought about the rehearsal she was missing. Checking her signal-less cell phone, she saw the time. Five fifteen. "So much for getting back in time for practice."

"Sorry."

"Oh, I forgot, you control the weather." She chuckled, hoping to lighten his mood.

"Cute."

"If they're able to have practice, at least someone will know we're out of pocket, and will try to call."

"Is Del in the band? I didn't recall him being the musical type."

"He's not. He always says if everyone were musicians, there wouldn't be an audience to applaud."

Nick chuckled as he walked. "Here's the tunnel leading to the old home place." He shone the light around the perimeter of the room. "The other tunnel has to be here somewhere."

There was a rock ledge, in deep shadow, off to one side. "Here it is." Lisa shone her flashlight behind the stone which was hiding the opening.

He turned his larger light to the opening and then back. When they'd come in from the bluff, the ledge hadn't appeared as prominent. "It looks different coming at it from this angle."

"Three tunnels leading to one room. Two bodies found. Let's hope there's not another." She laughed, but the shiver crawling up her spine still gave her the heebie-jeebies. "Stumbling upon one dead body per lifetime is enough for me."

"Agreed." He turned to her, tilting the flashlight to the ceiling for general lighting. "You ready?"

"Life has become an adventure since you came around, Nick." She gestured for him to proceed. "After you. Definitely."

He paused and grinned. "Is that a good thing or a bad thing?"

"I haven't decided yet." Was he thinking about earlier? About last night? It didn't take much to take her mind there, either.

He quirked an eyebrow at her and headed down the dark, narrow tunnel.

She grinned as she picked her way down the dark corridor of earth. "Have you noticed it's getting damper?"

"I have. It feels as if we're going uphill."

"Has to be. My legs are starting to burn." The ground seemed to be getting softer the further they got. "Do you smell that?"

"Yeah. Smells like freshly-plowed ground."

She tried to watch her step even as she watched the condition of the tunnel deteriorate on their way through. "Nick..."

"I know. We're stuck."

30

"I guess, over the years, the other part of the tunnel was maintained, and this part was forgotten." Nick shook his head. There was no way to get through this bog of mud and debris. He and Lisa had been through this section a few weeks ago. The idea that someone else had been in the tunnel with an eye to destruction shook him to the core.

"That could explain it." Lisa shone the light around the dead-end passageway. "Or, maybe this could." She picked up a broken piece of equipment and handed it to Nick.

"I don't think they had digital detonators in the late 60s, do you?" He stared at her in disbelief.

She shook her head and stared at him. "Someone closed off this part of the tunnel, and they did it for a reason."

He put the fragment in the pocket of his cargo shorts and turned the light back to the blocked passageway. "We won't figure that out today. Right now we need to find a way out of here."

Lisa pulled her phone from her pocket and checked for a signal. They had been going uphill. Maybe, just maybe...

She looked up at him in excitement. "I have a bar of signal."

"See if you can get a call out."

She punched in 9-1-1. "It's not connecting." Fear gripped her. "Do you think the tornado did damage in Marion?"

"It may have taken down the tower. Try sending a text to Del. It takes less signal."

She punched in a quick text to her brother. *SOS. We're trapped in the tunnel under Nick's house.*

Was it already six o'clock? She didn't realize they had been down there so long. She waited, relieved when she saw dots appear, indicating that he was reading or writing.

Are you OK? Damage is bad here, but I'm OK. I'll call somebody to get u out.

"He got it." She smiled up at Nick, so relieved she could have cried.

"Tell him we're in the tunnel where we have signal, but we'll go back closer to the basement of the house when we get word someone's on their way."

She tapped it in and held up her phone when she got Del's reply.

Get comfy. May take a while to get to you. Let you know when we're on our way.

Lisa sent him the "thumbs-up" emoji and smiled up at Nick. "Help is on the way."

Nodding, he pulled the piece of evidence from his pocket. "Somebody wanted this tunnel out of commission."

"Had to be whoever left the more recent body, don't you think?" She carefully took it from him, examining it in the palm of her hand to avoid messing up fingerprints.

"That would make sense."

She pulled a tissue from her pocket. "Wrap it up in this. Maybe it will keep any prints intact."

"You've watched your share of police drama, haven't you?"

"I have." She turned up her nose and inspected the muddy ground. "Del said to get comfy, but I refuse to sit in the mud."

"You have to be exhausted."

She huffed a little. "No more than you."

"I wasn't onstage this morning."

"It's not a stage, it's a platform." It wasn't like she was performing on Broadway.

"Same thing."

"Maybe. A little." She sighed. She was tired. Now that she knew help was on the way, her adrenaline level had evened out, and she could have taken a nap. But not here.

"We could use this time to get to know one another a little better." He lifted an eyebrow at her.

She shot him a look of curiosity mixed with reproach.

"I meant we could talk."

Now her face was red. She could feel it, and when he laughed out loud, she wanted to melt into the mud at her feet.

Nick calmed himself and reached out for her hand, leaning his back on the damp wall. "Tell me about Clay Lacey."

"What about him?" If he wanted to think she was pouting, she would give him all he wanted.

"You told me about your prom date, but you didn't tell me you and he had dated a few times in the last couple of years."

She shot him an even dirtier look. "Del."

"He's my source, yes."

How did you tell someone you might be falling in love with you had almost settled?

Was there any way to change the subject?

"Clay." She paused in thought. "I guess to tell you about Clay, I'd have to tell you about Michael."

He gaped at her, surprised. Del hadn't met Michael and didn't know how close she came to leaving home because of him.

"Who is Michael?"

"Michael and I dated while I was in Texas. He was on the crew of the show I was with."

"Was it serious?" There was a tiny frown between his brows.

"I thought so."

"What happened?"

"When Mom got sick, I wanted to come home immediately."

"Understandable."

"To you, maybe, and to Del, but not to Michael." She swallowed thickly, still feeling the hurt she'd felt when they parted. "He thought I should wait until things got worse, and I wanted to get in some quality time with my mom. Plus, Dad needed me, and Del did, too."

"How could he..."

"He wanted me to choose him over my family." She shrugged her shoulders. "I chose my family, and we haven't spoken since except when he called to tell me our bosses still had a spot for me if I wanted to come back."

"Was this after your mother passed?"

She nodded. "It was. He had not called, texted, sent flowers, cards, anything, the whole time Mom was in the process of dying."

He pulled her to him and hugged her. "I am so sorry."

She snuggled into his embrace and relaxed her face into his shoulder, hugging him back. Face hidden under his chin, she continued. "I thought he was the one, Nick."

She felt him nod as he tightened his embrace. "You dodged a bullet."

"I know." Her voice was muffled.

He leaned back to gaze into her eyes. "But that doesn't explain dating Clay."

"Oh, it really does, Nick." She stared at him, amazed she was even there, in his arms, discounting the situation they were in. "Clay was there when we were saying goodbye to Mom. He helped out, didn't demand my attention, and was good to me. I could almost have married him."

"He asked you to marry him?"

A chuckle worked its way out. "He really did. His timing wasn't great, but he did."

Closing his eyes, he shook his head. "Don't tell me..."

"Yep. He got down on one knee and proposed at the cemetery."

"It's different. I'll give him that."

"I told you he was a little awkward."

"Yes, but I give him props for knowing what he wanted."

"He didn't want me, he wanted to be married." She paused. "For that matter, so did I."

"Did you consider it?"

"For a fleeting moment, I did. I had left what I thought was the love of my life, and Clay was there, ready to adore me and give me anything I wanted." She shook her head. "And then I saw Del's face."

"He gave me an idea of what he thought about Clay, but he didn't tell me this part."

"Let me put it this way. Del looked pretty bad, anyway, because he'd just buried his mother."

"I can't even imagine."

"But when I saw him roll his eyes and shake his head. I wanted to laugh. I wanted to laugh out loud. At the cemetery. In front of all those people who were grieving with me."

"I'm sure your reaction didn't fill Clay with confidence."

"In retrospect, I feel sorry for him. And, I understand why he isn't one of my biggest fans."

"Oh, he's still watching out for you."

"Yeah, I know." She took a deep breath and picked at one of the buttons on his shirt, avoiding his eyes. "I came so close to settling. Sometimes I think I've settled all my life, but then I look back and see where those hard times were teaching me something. You know what I mean?"

"I do." He tightened his arms around her. "Hey."

She gazed up at him. His eyes were tender. Were those tears she saw hovering? Whether it was or not, she felt them begin in her own eyes. Great. As dirty as she was, tears would simply add to the amazing look she was sure she was pulling off.

"Hard times do teach us."

"It isn't fun at the time."

He shook his head and leaned down to kiss her lightly on her lips. "No, but if they bring us to this, it might be worth it."

"Do you think so?"

Not giving her a verbal answer, he gave her a thorough kiss. One she felt to her toes.

Oh, it was worth it, all right. Definitely worth it.

31

Nick felt the *buzz* and heard the *ding* of Lisa's phone in her pocket, but wasn't sure what it was for a few seconds. Honestly, he wasn't sure where he was at the moment until the sound broke through his own personal fog of desire.

When he lifted his head, Lisa looked up at him, a little cross-eyed, as if she couldn't see clearly for a few seconds. His kiss affected her that much. He hadn't fared much better. He stared down at her, still holding her close. He felt such a surge of surprise, and her face had an expression of elation, giving him a boost of confidence he hadn't felt in a long time. Their first kiss had been spectacular, but this? This was tending toward miraculous.

"You should probably check that."

"Check what?" She still looked shell-shocked—but in a good way.

"Your phone. I heard it ding." His grin grew as realization dawned on her face.

"Oh!" She pulled her arms from around him, her face rosy in the dim light. "Del says they're at the house."

"We need to make tracks, then."

"Hang on. He's sending another text, and if we get out of range, we'll lose it." She watched her phone, waiting for the series of dots to become words.

Nick picked up both flashlights and waited. He looked around, smiling as he thought about this place, this horrible, dirty, smelly place. He'd hold it in highest regard from now on.

"Here we go."

Kitchen floor joist blocking the door to the tunnel. Need more guys to move it. Go to opening on the other end. She closed her eyes, sick at the idea of the damage done in the house they'd been working on.

"Tell him to take some bolt-cutters to cut the lock."

She did, and then looked at him, her eyes round. "What if we're blocked going that direction?"

Nick clamped his lips together as he considered. "Tell him if we're not there in a half hour, we've been blocked that way."

As she texted the message to Del, she shook her head. "Surely they wouldn't close it off both ways."

"It would be more difficult. You could tell part had been used recently."

"Yeah, too recently if you ask me."

He tugged at her ponytail and grinned at her. "When we get the house finished, we'll make sure no one can get in the tunnel from anywhere other than the house."

"Sounds good. I would hate to think about getting up in the middle of the night and finding a criminal in my house."

He didn't say anything, but he smiled. She was picturing herself in the house. In his house.

"Did he get back to you?"

"He said, 'ten four.'"

"Good. Let's try to find our way to my great-grandparents' cellar."

At least it was dryer going back toward the main artery of the tunnel. Lisa looked down at her shirt and wrinkled her nose. She was surprised Nick hadn't taken one look at her and backed away instead of giving her the most amazing kiss of her life.

Walking behind him, his lean frame confidently leading the way, she wondered why, when men were covered in dirt and grime, they were somehow even more attractive.

But maybe it was just her. She felt her lips curve in a satisfied smile. Sure, her makeup was either all over her face or disintegrated, and the perfectly-straightened hair was in a ponytail and frizzed to its original curl, but it hadn't seemed to bother him.

She remembered Michael pointing out imperfections, and wondered why she thought he had the right to do so. It wasn't as if she had grown up with overly critical parents. In fact, sometimes she felt they went overboard the other way—handing out compliments when they weren't warranted. "Imposter Syndrome" strikes again.

Following behind Nick, she noticed how his hair tended to curl in the dampness, as did hers. He needed a haircut. When they were in college, he kept his hair short—she remembered a shaggy Del teasing him about his every-two-week hair appointments. When had he let it go? When Kristy died?

Maybe he'd decided there were more important things than outward appearances. It was something she had pondered all her life. She didn't want it to matter what other people thought, but it did, to her.

It especially mattered what Nick thought. She figured, to him, she was Del's little sister, and while he might be attracted to her physically, she could never meet the ideal that was his late wife. She shouldn't pin her hopes on an amazing, staggering, over-the-top kiss.

"Awfully quiet back there." Nick glanced over his shoulder and grinned. "You still behind me?"

"I'm still here, thinking."

"Me, too. Last time you followed me this close, we stumbled on a cat, kittens, and a corpse." He chuckled, the lighthearted sound soothing her worried soul.

"Ugh. Don't remind me. I'm all for an uneventful trek this time."

"We're almost there, and so far, so good."

"Do you think they'll be back?"

"Who?"

"Whoever killed the guy."

He walked on. "I would imagine they cut off that tunnel and deserted their lair, if you can call it that."

"Wow. You have a lair underneath your house." She felt a giggle bubble up. "Does this make you Batman?"

He looked back at her over his shoulder and lowered his voice to a rasp. "Maybe." Then he laughed out loud.

She wouldn't think about anything but getting out of there and what they needed to face on the outside. Worrying wasn't going to accomplish one thing. She'd have to learn to live one day at a time, like Nick had learned to do after losing Kristy.

"Do you think Alfred will have a hot bath drawn?"

"I hope so, although a shower might do more good."

When they arrived at the steps leading up to the site of the original Woodward homestead, she sighed loudly. "Thank You, Lord."

"Amen."

She checked her phone. One bar again. And a text from Del. *Heading up there. Tree across the lane.*

Nick read her text over her shoulder. "Must be pretty bad out there."

She tapped back: *We'll be at the steps waiting when you get here.*

Anxiety squeezed her heart as she gazed up at him, and he put his arms around her and held her again.

"Don't worry about it. We know Del's okay."

"I hope Darcy and the kids are all right." She didn't want to leave his arms.

"We'll check on them first thing when we get out." He pulled away and stared down at her, still keeping her in the circle of his arms. "There's something I want to say before Del and the others get here."

She started to pull away, but he tightened his grip, thank goodness. "Go ahead."

"I always knew you were special."

Nick knew what he needed to say, but he was afraid of botching it. His soul was at war within him and, to be honest, he was scared. The one thing he knew was he didn't want to let her go. Ever.

Lisa frowned. "In what way?"

He tilted his head, trying to put into words what was inside. "I knew you were beautiful, smart, kind, and had a funny streak, even when we were in college."

"I had everyone fooled." She was messing with that same button. It was going to come off if she didn't leave it alone. Not that he cared. He just wanted her close.

"No, you didn't."

"I'm nothing special, Nick. Really."

"Del warned me about this."

"What?" She stiffened in his arms. "You talked about me with my brother?" Now she was getting a little hot under the collar.

He tried to hide the grin. "I had to ask someone's permission to date you. Del was the only one available."

"Do you know how old I am?" She glared at him until what he said hit her full force, and then she seemed to soften in front of his eyes. "Date me?" She squeaked out the words.

Nick nodded, reveling in the feel of her relaxing into his arms.

"But I'm not..." She was cut off by his lips demanding her attention. He could, and would, stop any arguments she might have with his lips. That seemed fair.

"Yes you are," he mumbled, pausing for breath.

"But you were..." She was getting breathless, and he knew, by the sounds he could hear outside, he was running out of time to convince her.

"I was married."

She pulled her lips free and stared at him. "Yes, you were. Kristy..."

"Kristy was a woman I loved deeply. I always will."

He watched as she gazed at him, not saying anything. It was up to him.

"I didn't think God would give me a second chance to love someone, but He has."

"You..."

"Yes, Lisa, I do."

Suddenly a gust of air and a hail of debris came down on them. "Hey gang, help has arrived." Del was grinning, and four neighbors were behind him to help pull them up out of the cellar.

"Perfect timing, Del."

"I aim to please."

32

They emerged from the ground to see the sun setting in a clear sky. But the destruction was all around them.

Lisa hugged her brother as soon as she got up the steps. "You shouldn't be on that leg."

"You're welcome and so glad to see you, too." Del hugged her back, then turned to Nick. "There's a little damage to the house, but nothing that can't be fixed." He grimaced a little. "Your truck, on the other hand..."

"You're kidding."

Del shook his head. "You lost one of those big maples, right on the truck. It clipped the corner of the house, where the kitchen is, which is why there was damage to the basement. "I'm glad there was a tunnel, though. If you'd been in the basement, you might have been killed."

Lisa touched Nick on the arm. "I'm so sorry, Nick."

"It's all stuff." He threaded his fingers through hers and squeezed. "Stuff can be replaced. You can't." He looked down at her, and she knew, beyond a shadow of a doubt, that her face was flaming, and in front of her brother, of all people. Thank goodness it was nearly dark outside.

"O-kay..." Del's eyebrows were raised so high they were under his bangs, which perpetually needed to be cut.

"Hush, Del." She glared at him, still a little perturbed that Nick had discussed her love life with him.

Her brother twisted his lips, trying his best not to grin as he looked at Nick, who wasn't even trying to hide his smile.

"Oh, whatever." She huffed and walked over toward the other men heading to their truck, which was parked by Del's. Pulling out her phone, she noticed she had a minimal signal, so she sent Darcy a quick text before she turned toward her two men, hands on her hips. "We'll need a ride."

"As you wish, m'lady." Del bowed ridiculously and strode toward her, Nick on his heels.

The truck was a total loss. Nick pulled the picnic basket out of the back seat, avoiding the branches invading the space from the front of the cab being crushed.

"I wonder if the cookies survived." Lisa looked like she could use a cookie about now.

"Maybe, but getting to them might be tricky." He dreaded going inside the house. "Let's see what the damage is."

Sure enough, the enormous tree that landed on his truck also took out the electrical lines that hadn't been buried yet, and demolished the corner of the addition where the kitchen was. "At least we hadn't installed the restored windows yet."

"That would have been tragic."

He reached for Lisa when he noticed the floor. "Careful." Inside the back door, the floor began to give way, and by the time they got to the kitchen proper, the center floor joist had collapsed, wedging debris into the wall where the doorway to the tunnel was.

"I guess we need to add a few more weeks to the timeline." She gave him a sad little smile.

More time to work with her. "I can think of worse things." He smiled at her. They would continue their conversation from the tunnel, but not right now.

Del came back from checking out the rest of the house. "It seems that this is the only damage."

"You went upstairs?" Lisa frowned at her brother. "And where's your boot?"

"Ah, the doc told me last week I could start going without it."

"Yeah, but he also told you to wear it when you were going to be on your feet."

He waved her away. "He's being overcautious. I'm good. I was going to tell you I'm going to start work tomorrow." He shook his head at the mess in the kitchen. "Looks like it'll be all hands on deck."

"Unless there's more damage in town." Nick looked at them both. "I'd like to help if I can."

Lisa put a hand on Del's arm. "Have you heard from Darcy?"

"I called her before I came out to find you. She and the kids were at her mom's, over the restaurant, and they made it to the cellar under the building."

"That's a relief."

"Yeah. The twister missed the main drag, so there were a few barns blown away, and some trees, but nothing major." Del looked like he could use a chair, as much as he insisted he was okay.

"Let's get you back home, and if it's okay with Del, I'll clean up over at his house." Nick looked Del's way and nodded.

"I don't know if I want you to have any more heart-to-heart talks with my brother." Lisa arched an eyebrow at them both.

Del held up his hands in surrender. "So maybe my timing wasn't perfect?"

Lisa retrieved her purse, shook her head, and went to the truck, where she scooted into the middle and crossed her arms in a huff.

"Women, right?" Del winked at Nick.

"Oh yeah." Nick jogged to the truck and got in, then pulled Lisa close.

33

———————•◦•———————

Nick ripped open the envelope from the Kentucky state crime lab. The DNA test had required samples from himself, his dad, and the remains found in the tunnel. They had waited over two weeks for the results.

He had waited this long to see, but there was part of him that didn't want to know if the corpse found in the tunnel from the '60s was his grandfather or not.

At one time he had wondered if his dad's aloof parenting style would pass down to him. From what he'd heard, his grandfather was a tough old bird who wanted to raise a tough grandson. Was the old man's son a disappointment to him? Had he murdered his own son in cold blood? Had someone else killed him? Or had he given up and killed himself rather than carry on the tradition his father and grandfather had perpetuated before him?

If Granny were here, he could ask her about the men in his family. What little he knew came from her.

Pillars of the community and the local church, outlaws by trade. Whitewashed sepulchers.

The letter in his hand held some answers. He needed to know. Dad needed to know.

He reached in and grabbed the folded papers, surprised at the number of documents included. Scanning the letter on top, he read quickly, trying to get to the meat of it.

There it was: *The probability of the specimen being the biological*

*father of Daniel Woodward, Jr. is greater than 99.9999 %,
identifying it as Daniel Woodward, Sr.*

The numbers, the letters, all ran together as he tried to read it, but
that statement said it all. The skeletal remains in the tunnel belonged
to his grandfather, the man thought to have drowned in the Ohio River
in 1968.

Nick picked up the phone to call Dad, but called Lisa instead. Dad
got the same letter he did, so he'd wait and let Dad make the first move
this time. He'd resigned himself to the fact even before receiving
confirmation, but knowing he was part of a family that had not only
deceived the community, but had lived in such a way as to bring
murder to life made the doubts swirl.

"Hey." Lisa sounded happy to hear from him.

"Hey, yourself. What's happening in your little corner of the
world?" He wanted to hear something good.

"The tile guys are here and are setting tile in the bathroom
upstairs, and Del is here repairing plaster. All in all, a good day so far."

"Great. I'm running late, but I'll be there before lunchtime. I'm
checking on the lake house before I come up."

"That's fine. Want me to bring you a sandwich?"

"How about I bring sandwiches for you and Del?"

"Our Daily Bread?"

"Sure. Your usual?" He chuckled. Once she'd tried the curry
chicken salad on cranberry nut bread, she was hooked.

"You know it. And get Del the Southwest club."

"On jalapeño bread?"

"Oh, yes. He's sweating, but you know him. He doesn't consider
he's eaten Tex-Mex unless he's sweating from the inside, too."

"Gotcha." He paused a minute, wishing he were already there. "I
got the test results today."

Lisa interrupted him. "Let me get outside. You're breaking up."

"Go upstairs. The signal is better there."

"Oh yeah. Hang on."

He heard the stairs squeak with each step.

Lisa chuckled. "We still haven't gotten these steps quiet."

"I kinda like them that way."

"It would be great for parents of teenagers. You'd always know when they were going up and down the stairs."

If he had his way, he would someday know what that felt like. "I agree." He visualized her walking across to the large bank of windows in the generous master bedroom.

Her voice came across the airwaves. "So, are you still there?"

"I am. Can you hear me?"

"Much better. So?"

"The skeletal remains tested above ninety-nine percent that it was my grandfather, Daniel Woodward, Sr."

"Wow." She didn't say anything for a few seconds. "Have you talked to your dad?"

"Not yet." He craned his neck, looking up at the clouds in the sky. "I thought I'd let it soak in for both of us before we talked."

She was quiet. "Don't wait too long."

"I know." He nodded at the gentle reminder that he didn't know how much time he would have with his dad. "Yeah." He swallowed the lump in his throat. "Hey, I'll see you in about an hour, okay?"

"We'll be here. I'm trying paint samples so you can pick colors for me."

"Pick whatever you think will look good." Sometimes when he talked with her on the phone, he had a stab of regret, that internal voice telling him he wasn't worthy of someone like Lisa. Sometimes, like now, he simply wanted her. Badly. "See you in a bit."

"Be careful."

Lisa stood in the master bedroom staring down at her phone when Del caught up to her, covered in plaster and carrying his trowel.

"Hey, was that Nick?"

"Yeah, he's bringing sandwiches."

His eyes lit up at the thought. "Tex-Mex?"

"Yep. From Our Daily Bread. Sound good?"

"Delectable. Although Darcy's Tex-Mex sandwich is every bit as good."

"We need to get her to start making her own bread." Lisa locked her phone and stuck it in her back pocket. "I think she's been experimenting a little since Dad and Roxy got home."

"She's as good a cook as Roxy."

Lisa nodded, then realized Del wasn't just standing there to discuss lunch plans. "Whatcha need?"

"Mr. Fisher is here with the windows, and he's bringing them in to install. They look awesome." Del nodded with enthusiasm.

"Great! That will be some good news for Nick today." She started down the stairs. "Have the wooden storms come yet?"

"No, but they did say six-to-eight weeks since they're custom."

She rushed into the dining room, where the first windows were being placed. The wavy glass was fastened securely, broken panes replaced with identical glass from the old storm windows. She couldn't help it. She did a little happy dance. "They're amazing."

Mr. Fisher and his sons smiled. "Glad you approve of them."

"Nick will love them."

The bearded older gentleman pushed his hat back in the August heat, nodding. His plain attire bespoke his Amish heritage, but the twinkle in his eyes showed a kindred spirit. He loved the "old stuff," too.

"They were nice windows. No rot. They needed to be tightened up, reglazed, and the ropes replaced. Used all the old weights. We had a couple left from where you're putting in the French doors in the back, and I left them on the front porch. Thought you might want to keep them."

"Thank you. I don't know if Nick has ever seen them before. He's mostly done new construction." She shook her head along with the crew, and they chuckled together.

Mr. Fisher grinned. "He has missed out."

Lisa smiled and said "Excuse me" to the Fishers when the phone vibrated in her pocket. When she pulled it out, she saw it was Mel. "Hey, girl. Are you okay?"

"I'm fine, I'm two weeks past my due date, and I'm irritable, but that's all about to change."

"Are you in labor?" She wanted to squeal, but knew Mel hadn't just called to shoot the breeze.

"Finally. Listen, I can't find Jake. He's helping Dad with one more push to get hay in before he has to get back in school. I had a doctor's appointment, and he's admitting me into the hospital. Apparently I've been having contractions all day and didn't realize it."

Lisa could hear Mel groan. "Are you okay?"

"I'm fine. Another contraction. It's like this little one woke up this morning and decided it was time since Daddy's out in the boonies with Granddad."

"Is your mom there with you?"

"She is, so I'm fine. I just need you to find Jake. I think he's over at the farm on Hebron Church Road. You know, the one with the white house?"

"I know the one. I'll head over there. Won't take me five minutes to get there from here."

"Good. Tell him to bring my bag."

"Got it."

"And for goodness' sakes, tell him to take a shower before he comes."

Lisa laughed. "Will do. Keep me posted?"

"You know I will. And I expect visitors tonight."

"Yes, ma'am." She saluted, even though Mel couldn't see her. "I will see you tonight."

<hr />

Lisa finally relaxed. "It's been a big day already, and it's barely noon."

She, Del, and Nick lounged on the front porch eating their sandwiches, and the crew was spread out in various places on their lunch break as well. No hammering or sawing for a brief time, the birdsong taking over.

"Did you have any trouble finding Jake?" Nick asked between bites of his Cubano sandwich.

"No. He was exactly where she said he would be, but there wasn't the least bit of signal out there. Jake and her dad won't hear the end of it, I'm sure.

"I wouldn't want to be in their shoes."

"Me, neither." Lisa wadded up her sandwich wrappers and put it in the bag they came in. "Would you like to go with me to visit them in the hospital tonight?"

A strange expression crossed his face. Surely he had been to a hospital since Kristy's accident.

"If you don't want to, that's fine. I thought maybe we could go down early enough to pick up the pedestal sink for the downstairs bathroom. I got a call it was in."

"That sounds good." He smiled at her, his visage clearing. It was possible that his last experience resulted in the death of his wife and unborn child, and she was asking him to go and visit a newborn. She could have kicked herself.

On the other hand, if you don't put yourself out there to experience life, you can't recover from what it's thrown at you.

"Let's look at those paint samples. After I told you to pick, I had visions of purple walls."

"Very funny. As if. Now for a house this age, mustard was a big color. Also known as 'ochre.'"

"No thank you."

She nodded. "Follow me, then."

He winked at her. "Any time, any place." He pulled himself up from the glider and looked down at Del, dozing, the bill of his ball cap covering his eyes. "I'm glad you don't work by the hour."

"Yeah, I'm thinking about changing our pay structure. I think a paid siesta would be good for morale."

Lisa pulled the screen door wide. "Enjoy it while you can. Once I get ready to paint, all bets are off." After she entered, she let the old-fashioned screen door slam on purpose.

34

The last time Nick had entered Western Baptist Hospital was the night his whole world collapsed. Somehow he'd been able to avoid it. He knew how. He'd made himself a hermit in his off-work hours.

It was different, walking in through the automatic front doors. The soaring ceiling encompassing three stories of the hospital was a far cry from the bustling ER he'd seen last time. He looked down when he felt Lisa's hand take his. "Hey."

"Are you sure this is okay?" Her eyes seemed to peer into his soul.

"I'm fine. I had to come here sometime." He squeezed her hand and gave her a nervous smile.

"We don't have to stay long." She seemed nervous, too. "When Mel's Emily was born, I was in Texas."

"We'll stay as long as we need to." They entered the elevator, and when the door closed and they were alone, he pulled her into his arms for a hug. "Mel's your best friend, and Jake's my cousin. We're family."

She leaned back in his arms and smiled up at him. The doors opened to the second floor and the nursery area.

Music was playing in the hallway and everyone seemed excited.

"What's going on?" Why were they playing music? Wouldn't that get old after a while?

"They play music when a baby's been born." She chuckled. "They've been doing it for a long time. I remember when Mom was in the hospital here, we would hear the music play and it was nice, you know?"

"What room are they in?"

"Two oh five, so it should be right around the corner."

They came upon the partially-closed door and Lisa knocked gently.

Jake stuck his head out the door and opened it wide, then hugged Nick and Lisa both, his excitement infectious. "The grandparents just left. Come in and meet the little prince."

Nick hung back as Lisa approached the throne, otherwise known as the hospital bed, where Melanie and little Samuel held court. What was it with women and new babies? He watched with interest as Lisa's shoulders went up in excitement, and a little squeal came from her as she rushed to hug Mel and inspect the baby.

"Oh, Mel, he's amazing."

"Isn't he? I think I did rather well, considering the father of my child almost missed the birth." Her smile belied the sharpness of her tone.

Jake walked over to the bedside. "We have you to thank that I didn't miss it all, Lisa. Thanks for coming to find me."

"I was happy to do it." Lisa looked over at Nick, a question in her eyes.

He walked closer, peering at the newborn.

"Would you like to hold him?" Jake deftly picked up the tiny baby and offered him to Nick.

"Oh, I couldn't..."

He glanced at Lisa, who was smiling at him tenderly. "Go ahead, because once I get my hands on him, you might not get another chance." She was teasing, but not.

The infant barely filled Nick's hands. He was amazing. This tiny human, who, twelve hours ago, was safely inside his mother's womb, was a person named Samuel. As Nick got used to the feel of the baby, he tucked him in the crook of his arm and began to sway.

"You're a natural." Lisa put her hand on his arm and stood there next to him, gazing at the precious child.

He had spent a lot of time over the last few years being angry. Angry at Kristy for leaving him. Angry at God for allowing it. Angry at his parents—Dad for lying to him, and Mom for her part in the lies.

Sometimes he was even mad at Lisa for pulling him out of his funk.

But now? He looked up at Jake and Melanie, at Lisa, and then back down at Sam—he'd call him Sam, of course—and simply felt thankful.

"You're hogging the baby." Lisa stood there, grinning, but there were tears in her eyes. They were happy tears, and it wouldn't take much for him to produce some, too.

Lisa finally got her hands on that perfect little bundle of love. She would admit, watching Nick holding Samuel so easily did things to her insides she knew she would never forget.

She began to talk to little Sam. "Sweetheart, I'm your Aunt Lisa. Someday I'll have kids, too, and I'm going to need you to teach them how to get along in the world. Is that okay?"

"Um, is there something we should know?" Melanie laughed.

"No, I'm talking about hypothetical children." She knew her face was getting red, so she hid it in the baby blanket. She didn't dare look at Nick. For him to have been so nervous earlier, all it took was a little new baby smell and he seemed as happy as a lark.

And he couldn't seem to keep his eyes off of her. Or maybe he was looking at Sam. She got up the nerve to glance at him with a serene smile and felt a boost when she saw his color rise for a change.

Sam started fidgeting, his tiny mewling cry indicating distress. "Is he hungry?"

"I'm sure. Where Emily couldn't stay awake long enough to get in a good meal, this fella wants it all the time." Melanie held her arms out to take the baby, who had pulled out all the stops and began to bellow his frustration.

After reluctantly giving Sam back to his mother, she put her hand on Nick's arm. "We should go." She knew Mel would like privacy to nurse her baby, and it had been a big day for all of them. They had to be tired. "When do you think you'll go home?"

Jake stood up to walk them out. "The doctor said tomorrow if everything goes okay tonight."

"I'll let you know when we get home." Melanie paused in getting herself and Sam situated. "Thanks for coming, guys. It means a lot."

"I wouldn't have missed it for the world." Lisa rushed over and kissed her friend on the cheek. "Love you, Mel. I'll bring you brownies."

"Love you, too, Lis, and you'd better."

35

Nick noticed Lisa was quiet as they drove back to Crittenden County. She'd been lost in thought, barely saying a word from Paducah to the lakes area. "Penny for them?"

"My thoughts?"

"No, your brownies." He gave her a look and grinned. "You've been quiet since we left the hospital."

"I know."

They drove on a little ways, and Lisa took a deep breath and spoke. "I should have brought my truck up and left it at your house so you wouldn't have to make the trip all the way there and back."

"I don't mind." Any time he could spend with her, he certainly didn't mind. "Thanks for asking me to go with you."

"I didn't want to go alone." Her face was serious. Sad, even.

"It's for sure I wouldn't have gone if you hadn't." He gave her a half smile.

"I know." She took a deep breath and sighed. "I keep thinking about Mom."

"When you have kids?"

"Yes. She won't be there."

He pulled the truck into a lot overlooking Barkley Lake. The sun was setting, and the air was still. When he had turned off the truck and opened the windows, he took her hand into both of his. "It stinks."

There were tears in her eyes. "Yeah, it does." Then she gave a short laugh, staring straight ahead as if she didn't want to face him. "But it doesn't even compare to what you've gone through." She seemed frustrated.

"Hey." He pulled her chin toward him. "It does so compare."

She shook her head. "No. You lost a wife. A child."

"And you lost your mother. Someone you'd had all your life."

"I watched Dad when he lost Mom. He crumbled, Nick. Simply crumbled." Tears were pouring, now. "When I think about you in the same position, it hurts too much. I can't stand the thought that you had to go through the same thing."

He took her into his arms, where they sat, both of them crying. "Do you know what I thought before I knew I was attracted to you?"

Muffled, she spoke in his shoulder. "What?"

"That I didn't deserve a second chance to love someone."

She lifted her head and glared at him with fury. "Nicolas Woodward, how could you even think such a thing?"

He grinned. "Because I had lost someone I was supposed to love, honor, and cherish. Part of that is protection, and I couldn't protect Kristy. And then, guess what?"

"What?"

"I met a girl who falls through porches and runs into coffee tables on a regular basis."

"That would be me." She fussed with the tissue in her hand, then looked up at him with a hint of a smile.

"Yes, that would be you." He tilted his head and stared deeply into her eyes. "I also met your dad."

"Who had been crushed, and survived." She sniffed loudly.

"Yes. I had spent the last two years hiding out."

"Like Elijah running from Jezebel."

He laughed. "Well, not quite, but I get your point. What I meant was, I spent the last two years hiding out, and your dad taught me that

God gives us these times of trouble to show us how much He loves us."

He took both her hands. "Hey, look at me." Her swimming eyes threatened to take him out. "We've both lost someone very dear to us. It's easy to think we're the only ones, but we aren't. Everybody hurts at one time or another."

"When God allows hurt, he also gives us healing." She nodded. "I'm sorry to be such a blithering idiot."

"I refuse to let anyone call the woman I love a blithering idiot. Got it?"

She gave him a half smile, her face blooming a delicious rosy color. "Got it."

"I love you, Lisa Reno, and I'm tired of letting the past rise up to haunt us."

"I love you, Nick Woodward. Can I kiss you now?"

His face creased in a smile that threatened to take over as he pulled her into his arms. "I would be very upset if you didn't."

So she did.

36

SEPTEMBER

"I can't believe you kicked me out of my own house."

Lisa smiled into the phone. "If there's one thing I learned working on Home TV, it's the value of a good 'reveal' at the end of a project."

"We're almost there." Nick sounded excited.

"Good. I miss you." She looked down the lane to see Del's truck arriving, Nick in tow.

He got out of the truck, flowers in hand. Why had he brought flowers?

"I missed you, too." Nick handed her the bouquet and took her in his arms, kissing her tenderly. "It's been a whole week, you know."

She savored his lips, smiling, and he spoke to her, their foreheads touching. "It's been a long week."

"All right, you two." Del huffed.

Lisa twisted her lips in a rueful smile and turned toward her brother. "Thank you for bringing him home, Del."

"You're welcome, Highness."

"Now, Nick, stand beside me and focus on your new front elevation."

"Very nice. The landscaping looks fantastic."

"It needed some work after the tornado. I am so sad about the big maple, but now you can have plants that enjoy a little sun." She tilted her head, looking at the property from every angle.

"Good point." He turned her toward him once more. "As much as I want to see what you've done to the house, I have something to say."

She felt butterflies fighting one another for space in her tummy. Surely not. Not now. Confusion flew in and made her speechless. But he hadn't asked the question yet, so she wasn't supposed to be speaking. Not yet, anyway. But when he did speak, what would he say? And what would *she* say?

Perfect love casts out all fear.

Okay, young lady, pull up your big-girl pants and see what the man has to say before you get all tongue-tied when you're not supposed to be talking anyway. He may want to ask you a question about the gutters.

"Lisa." He tilted his head to catch her sight-line and get her attention. "Earth to Lisa." He laughed.

"Sorry. You had something you wanted to say?"

"At least one thing. Maybe more. We'll see."

She swallowed thickly. "You have my undivided attention."

"Good. First, I hope you don't mind having me in the neighborhood, because I've decided to move into the house."

"Oh good!" That made her happy. "When are you moving in?"

"It depends on the other things I want to say."

"Okay." She imitated zipping her lips, locking them, and throwing away the key.

"Second, Del has asked if I would be interested in going into business with the two of you, but I said only if you agreed. I don't want to butt in where I'm not wanted."

She felt herself jumping, but she finally figured out it was on the inside. So she nodded with enthusiasm.

"Got it."

Her heart threatened to explode when he got on one knee. He took the flowers from her hands and laid them carefully on the ground beside him, then took both of her hands in his. "I have a third statement, and it has a follow up question. May I proceed?"

She nodded slowly.

"Lisa Elizabeth Reno. I love you more than I ever thought I could love anyone. I probably could have loved you a long time ago, but I wasn't ready, and you weren't either. God once blessed me with a wonderful wife, and I loved her. He took her away, but He brought me to you, and I can't imagine my life, from here on out, without you in it. Will you give me a second chance?" He stared into her eyes which were filled with tears. "Will you marry me and help me fill this house up with more Woodwards?"

She thought her face would split open when she smiled. It had to be freakishly big, but the tears in her eyes were happy tears, not hurt, sad, or angry tears. She pulled her hands from his and put them on his face. "I would love to marry you, Nick Woodward."

From somewhere he produced a ring that he slipped easily on her finger. After kissing the hand that wore his diamond, he rose up and pulled her into his arms, his lips finding the crease between her shoulder and neck as he picked her up off her feet and held her close. "You have no idea how happy you've made me."

Once he had set her back on her feet, Lisa reached up to wipe the tears from his face, finally feeling the freedom to stand there, in his arms, knowing that maybe, just maybe she deserved the love of this man.

"How many kids can we have?"

He threw his head back and laughed, then settled her closer to him. She could feel him all along her body. "As many as you want, my dear. If we need more room, I know some amazing contractors who could be available to finish the attic."

"Good, because I don't think three bedrooms is going to be

enough." She smiled at him smugly, relishing the glint in his eye as he leaned down to kiss her as thoroughly as she could stand.

And maybe a little more.

Between kisses, Lisa prayed for a short engagement.

The End

A NOTE FROM THE AUTHOR

It has been a joy to share a little bit of my community with you through this story.

In 1991, we moved sixty miles from our hometown of Symsonia, Kentucky to Marion, Kentucky, little knowing, thirty years later, that it would be the place we would raise our children and create a life. Crittenden County is home to a population of 9,200, and the county seat, Marion, mentioned in the story, has a population of approximately 3,000.

I've tried to be as accurate as possible about the town and the roads in the county.

What is fictional, however, is Clementville–but not completely! In the early 1800s, there was a Clement family (their descendents still live in the area) in which the patriarch dreamed of creating a town on the river called "Clementburg." Sadly, he died in a sawmill accident much like the story about Nick's ancestor who wanted to found "Salinaville," which is totally fictional.

I have placed Clementville in the area between the Cave-In-Rock ferry landing on the Crittenden County side of Kentucky, and Riverfront Park upriver to the east, which is where the old "Dam 50" was located.

It's a beautiful part of the county with rolling hills and river views. We have a thriving Amish community, and most families run greenhouses, cabinetmaking shops, stores and other businesses.

There is a blogger I mention when Nick decides to restore his antique windows, and it is Scott Sidler's "The Craftsman Blog," https://www.thecraftsmanblog.com. If you're interested in restoration and "old stuff," check it out!

I hope you enjoy this glimpse into my home county, and into the lives of the Reno family. Stay tuned!

Thank you for reading,

Regina Rudd Merrick

Psalm 37:4

ACKNOWLEDGMENTS

In any writing project, there are many to thank.

First, I want to thank my husband, Todd, for his love, encouragement, and willingness to take on household tasks when I need to hole up in my office. I have been so blessed. He has even allowed me to ignore him from time to time when he was bursting to talk to someone, ANYONE, during the COVID-19 crisis.

My grown-up daughters and son-in-law—Ellen, Emily and Ben—for their patience with their mother who probably hasn't been as attentive as she would like. By the way, they're all writers too!

My extended family—especially my parents and in-laws. They're so excited to have a published author in the family, and are so careful to not take up time that could be spent writing. I love you all dearly!

My Mosaic family—you have encouraged, prodded, and loved me when I didn't think I could finish, due to crazy family things going on. You helped me get this done through a wedding, a parental hospitalization, and a pandemic! Wow!

My editor, Lesley Ann McDaniel, for your kindness and amazing advice. It's hard to switch editors, and you made it so easy!

My writing groups—KenTen and CCPL—I love you all so much. You have no idea how wonderful it is to have you to run things by, and to just get me out of my own head to focus on *your* writing!

And finally, to my Lord and Savior, Jesus Christ. I wasn't sure if this novel would happen, but when I found myself channeling anxiety and tears through my characters' prayers, I knew He was with me. He gives His peace, His love, and His rest. Thank You, Heavenly Father!

ABOUT THE AUTHOR

Regina Merrick began reading romance and thinking of book ideas as early as her teenage years when she attempted a happily-ever-after sequel to *Gone with the Wind*. That love of fiction parlayed into a career as a librarian, and ultimately as a full-time writer. She began attending local writing workshops and continued to hone her craft by writing several short and novel-length fan-fiction pieces published online, where she met other authors with a similar love for story, a Christian worldview, and happily-ever-after.

Married for thirty-five plus years and active in their church, Regina and her husband have two grown daughters who share her love of music, writing, and the arts. They live in a hundred-year-old house in Marion, Kentucky.

Connect with Regina through her website at https://www.reginaruddmerrick.com, Facebook, Instagram, Goodreads, and Bookbub.

BOOKS BY REGINA RUDD MERRICK

Southern Breeze Series

Carolina Dream

Carolina Mercy

Carolina Grace

Coastal Promises

(novella collection that includes "Pawley's Aisle," a Southern Breeze
Story)

The Mosaic Collection

Hope is Born

(Novella collection that includes "RenoVating Christmas,"
a RenoVations Story)

RenoVations Book 1: *Heart Restoration*

Coming in June 2021

RenoVations Book 2!

Coming soon to

THE MOSAIC COLLECTION

Pieces of Granite by Brenda S. Anderson

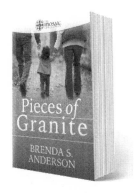

A distressing diagnosis
A retreating husband
A prodigal brother

Marriage counselor Debbie Verhoeven excels at piecing broken families together, so she never imagined her own perfect family could be fractured.

When Debbie learns the child she's carrying has Down syndrome, she takes the news in stride, but her husband, Jerry, begins suffering debilitating panic attacks that strike at his marriage, family, and faith.

Struggling to hold her family together, Debbie turns to her older brother for support, but he suggests the unthinkable. With no one else to turn to, her once-strong faith begins to crumble.

For the first time in her life, Debbie needs someone to lean on, but who is left to be strong for her?

Made in the USA
Columbia, SC
01 September 2020